Devil's Reef

A Harry McCoy Mystery

by

D. E. Karlson

DEDICATION

For Emma, Norman and Dougie

PROLOGUE

The Straits of Florida
April, 1916

The submarine pitched and rolled in the storm. Wind shrieked through the steel rigging, and spray stung the skipper's face as he looked out at the massive swells. He tightened his grip as a monstrous wall of green water broke over the bow and smashed into the bridge. The Wilhelmshaven shuddered, her twin diesels at full power, then slowly pulled herself from the sea's grasp.

Korvettenkapitan Manfred Augersbeck had been on the bridge for two hours and was drenched, the saltwater finding a way beneath his oilskins and into his boots. Still, he thought, better on the bridge than down below, at least a man could see what was coming.

The sub's bow heaved up on the slope of the next wave, this time slicing through the breaking crest. She slammed down into the black trough, then surged back up again. The captain leaned toward the hatch as the navigation officer shouted up at him.

"Barometer down two tenths, wind fifty knots!"

The distraction annoyed him, he didn't need junior officers telling him what he already knew.

"What about flooding?" he shouted back.

"The pumps are keeping up, barely."

The vessel had begun leaking twelve hours earlier, partially flooding the forward compartments. Before continuing across the Atlantic, they had to find a quiet inlet

1

to make repairs.

Aboard the American tramp steamer Josiah Long, Captain Nathanial Gurnee had his own set of problems to consider. Number two engine was running at reduced power, limiting speed and rudder response. It, too, needed repairs, but they would have to wait; a storm was not the time to take an engine off line. Gurnee had hoped to have completed his business and be in Havana by now -- instead, he was hove to in a storm, waiting. So they would make the rendezvous in the morning, after the seas had settled. Then, by his estimation, he would be in Havana by nightfall. The alarm from the starboard watch jarred him from his thoughts.

"Man overboard!"

"It's Anderson!" someone yelled.

"Turn on the lights," ordered the captain automatically. The search beams came on. "Christ, not Anderson," he thought as he ran to the starboard flying bridge. Blinding spray lashed at his face. Mountains of water towered over the freighter, and Anderson was out there, somewhere. He must have slipped coming up the ladder on his way back from the engine room, thought Gurnee. The captain squinted at the howling sea.

"Hard right rudder!" he shouted. There wasn't time to do anything else but what had been drilled into him since his days as a midshipman at the maritime academy. But what were the chances in these waters? What hope of rescue? Still, every seaman had heard stories of men washed away by one wave, and back aboard by another. It would be a miracle, but they had to try.

The captain noted the ship's heading, making a mental calculation to determine when he should order the rudder shifted again so they would arrive back at their original position. Slowly, the ship came into the wind, her two-thousand tons listing dangerously as she presented her beam to the waves.

Back aboard the Wilhelmshaven, visibility had gotten worse. The sub was too low, caught in the ocean's froth as waves heaved up in great walls. Only from the crests could the crew see through the rain and spray, a hundred and fifty feet at best. When the lookout spotted the Josiah Long, it was too late. The tramp steamer was turning, being pushed sideways by the waves.

"Hard-a-starboard!   Full   speed!" screamed Korvettenkapitan Augersbeck into the brass speaker tube. The steamer's massive bow caught them square amidships. There was no time to launch life rafts, no time to escape the stricken vessel. The sound of the impact, of crushing hulls, drowned out the fury of the storm, if only for a few moments. The Wilhelmshaven rolled on her side, then disappeared into the tortured sea.

Aboard the steamer, there was no mistaking the sound of ripping steel; the crew listened in horror as it reverberated though the hull. It was the sound of death.

The Josiah Long lasted longer than the Wilhelmshaven. Panic stricken, the crew launched the ship's three lifeboats, only to watch them swamped and smashed against the side of the ship. She drifted for miles, sent distress signals, but received no reply. She began listing to starboard, further, further, as wave after wave battered her. The crew could do nothing but hold on, wait for it to stop, wait for her to come back up. But the further she rolled, the more certain it became that she would not, could not, right herself. Her bow sank ever deeper as the ocean poured through the mortal gash ripped in the hull. When the final wave washed over her side, nothing remained but the sea.

3

ONE

Miami, Present day

He was dead before he hit the water.

I knew that because he was still floating. Drifting out into the bay, in fact. So he must have stopped breathing, because his lungs hadn't filled with water. He was fat, too, and that helped. Fat is buoyant.

My hands were shaking and I think I was having palpitations. All these years and I'd never killed a man before. I went into the cabin and poured myself a shot of vodka and then waited for the police to show.

I'd come to Miami for some much needed, doctor recommended R and R, and instead it was like I'd stumbled onto the set of "Scarface." The next think I knew I was standing on the dock and a cop was shining a flashlight in my face, then at the body in the water.

"Who is he?"

"The other one called him Demetri."

"There were two?"

I nodded.

"So where's the other?"

"He ran away."

The officer pointed his flashlight back in my face. "Demetri, what is that, Greek?"

I shook my head. "Russian, I think."

"You shot him?"

"Yep."

"He's dead?"

I looked out again at the body. He was floating face down now, still not moving. "I'm not a doctor, but yes, I'm guessing yes."

"What's your name?"

"Harry McCoy."

"You live here?"

I nodded.

"So what happened?"

"He tried to shoot me, I fired back."

"You better start at the beginning."

The beginning was twelve hours earlier, one of those scorching Miami afternoons that made you wonder if the Earth wasn't off course somehow, drifting too close to the sun. It was hurricane season, and we were already into the G's. Tropical Storm Gus. It didn't sound too dangerous, but then what did I know?

Somewhere off the coast of Africa another storm called Henrietta was whipping up. The weathermen were watching both of them, Gus and Henrietta, and school children tracked them with felt tipped pens and plastic laminated charts they got free at the supermarket.

I was dehydrated, and thinking about an ice-cold Coke as I motored slowly across the harbor toward the boatyard. The wake from the boat on the smooth water looked like a funhouse mirror. Hot air rippled off the concrete pier where a young man in coveralls worked a rusty red diesel pump, mopping his forehead with a dirty bandanna.

Carefully adjusting the throttle, I reduced speed until Hobo, my 36-foot Hong Kong built yawl, couldn't go any slower without stopping. Then I steered in a wide arc to bring her alongside the dock, where I killed the engine and stepped off the boat, line in hand. Textbook. The motorboat tied up ahead of me was called Rum Runner, spelled out in gold lettering on 45 feet of shiny blue gel coat, stainless steel, and mahogany trim. A yacht club burgee, red with a white trident, dangled limp on the bow. On the stern deck, the engine hatch was open, revealing a powerful Caterpillar diesel engine. A young man in his mid-twenties with longish blond hair was on his hands and knees working on the engine. He had the weathered look of someone who'd been at sea for a while, bleached and dried out by sun and salt and wind. He wore a blue polo shirt with the name of the boat stitched on the breast. Very fancy. A second man with the same shirt paced up and down the dock. Everything was all matchy-matchy. I figured he was the owner. He had on dark glasses and a baseball cap but I could see just enough of his face to make me think I knew him. He recognized me first.

He took off his sunglasses, "Harry?"

I hadn't seen Evan Salisbury in a long time. We'd been friends in college, back in Evanston, though I wouldn't say close. He was heir to a real estate fortune, and from what I had heard, was now a South Florida business magnate. I was an out-of-work lawyer, and not looking to change that any time soon.

"Harry McCoy," he pumped my hand, a grin breaking across his face. "It must be 20 years."

Evan Salisbury looked very much as I remembered him. He was still tall, which you would expect, and still skinny, which was an exception to the rule. He had the same curly brown hair, cut shorter than I remembered, a deep tan, and on the whole, the look of a man who was doing well.

"I was just at the reunion. You didn't go."

6

I wrinkled my nose and shook my head. I was having a mid-life crisis, actually it was a lot more than that, and not interested in sharing. Too many questions, too much explanation. Evan started going through the roster of our fraternity house, reminiscing and laughing. For a moment I was worried he was going to break into the old football fight song.

"So what brings you here?" he asked.

"Getting ice."

"No, I mean Miami."

"I'm en route to the islands," I said. "Waiting for the weathermen to give me the go ahead. Looks like you guys have been somewhere."

He hesitated. "Fishing out near Bimini, just got back. Now I'm looking for place to tie up." He lowered his voice and raised his hand to his mouth, "need to put some sea room between me and my wife, we're getting a divorce and she practically lives at the club where I keep the boat."

"Goddamit!" The crewman threw his wrench on to the deck. He'd pinched his fingers.

"What's wrong with your boat?"

He made a dismissive wave. "Who knows."

The crewman looked up at Evan. "Try it now."

Evan hopped aboard and turned the ignition, the engine wouldn't turn over.

The crewman threw his rag at the engine. "Son-of-a-bitch!"

"Fuel is usually the problem, is there fuel in the separator?" I asked.

"Yeah."

"How does it look?"

He poked his head down into the engine compartment. "It looks dirty."

"Then you probably have contaminated fuel."

I spent a half hour showing him how to drain and refill the fuel separator. A year earlier, I'd known next to nothing about boats, in fact I had always been mechanically challenged, or maybe just not interested. Never changed an oil filter or anything like that. But I did have good survival instincts, and knew the boat was the only thing between me and the Atlantic Ocean. I'd watched enough episodes of Shark Week to know it was important the boat never sank.

I found I enjoyed the mechanical systems on the boat: the plumbing for the head, the stove, the fresh water system, the radio, and the bilge pump. My doctor said it was good therapy. I'd left the DA's office after a breakdown, I guess you'd call it, though the doctors didn't. Acute reactive disorder, anxiety, depression, I think, were the words they used. Nothing that $350 worth of prescription anti-depressants a month couldn't help. I'd taken the pills for a while. Then I bought the boat, and stopped taking the pills.

I still woke in the middle of the night, the usual symptoms – anxiety, panic, cold sweats. That's when I would pull out my book on boat maintenance. And so I'd learned about diesel engines.

When we finished with the fuel separator, the young crewman, whose name was Andrew, started the engine. It coughed to life. I was more impressed than they were. I bought my ice and Salisbury helped me load it aboard Hobo.

"So, where do you keep your boat?" he asked.

"I'm tied up at a marina not far from here, Biscayne Towers."

"You think there's room for me?"

"Gee, I don't know…."

"I'll call them."

"They're usually pretty full.   They probably won't answer the phone."

"Doesn't hurt to try."

TWO

Rum Runner arrived at Biscayne Towers later that afternoon. It was raining, the usual showers that roll in from the Everglades in the late afternoon in the summer, the big drops dimpling the surface of the water in the marina, splattering on the deck above me. I was frying sweet Italian sausages in Hobo's cabin. For some reason the pan was smoking like hell. The more butter I put in the pan, the more it smoked. The smoke couldn't vent from the galley because the hatch was closed, and the smoke and smell of sausages filled the cabin as I bent down to get a better look through the porthole. The gray shape of Salisbury's boat materialized like a ghost through the fog. I pulled on my slicker, turned off the stove and went topsides.

Salisbury was at the helm as Rum Runner motored up to the dock. Andrew threw me a line and Salisbury helped tie up. When he was satisfied, he surveyed his new surroundings. You couldn't see much because it was raining. He squinted under his waterproof hood.

Biscayne Towers was an apartment complex catering mostly to business travelers who wanted furnished executive flats with maid service, and rich South Americans on shopping sprees. The marina was an afterthought. It was less expensive than the big marinas, and more secluded. As a bonus, there was a large swimming pool that was never crowded. Next to it was a garden with banyan trees drenched in Spanish moss, and the entire property was surrounded by a weathered cement and stucco wall. I'd thought it seemed a good place to hole up for a while.

Salisbury liked it too. "Seems quiet, that's good, that's very good. I think I'll like it," he said, and I pointed him to the marina office to do the paperwork.

The sausages were hopelessly burned, so I went out to a Chinese restaurant. When I returned the marina was quiet, and I spent the rest of the evening reading a fishing tackle catalog. It started raining again, and as I lay in my bunk I listened to the rip of thunder in the distance, and the gentle gurgling of water draining from the gutters of the harbormaster's office. Somewhere a steel halyard was slapping frantically against an aluminum mast. It was driving me nuts, so I closed all the portholes and turned on the air conditioner. Around midnight I fell asleep.

When I woke the wind and rain had stopped. So had the air conditioner. The cabin was hot and airless, and I was thirsty. I climbed out of my bunk and opened the main hatch and then filled a cup with water. I stood in the companionway breathing in the fresh night air, then returned to my bunk and tried to sleep. I listened to the engine noise of a shrimp boat motoring in its usual curly-cues around the bay. The shrimper had been working the waters near the marina for the past several days, using a lantern to attract the shrimp.

I heard the slow tentative squeak of the marina gate. Someone tripped, and then cursed.

A hushed voice. "Who leaves a hose out?"

"Shhh."

The sound of the shrimper wasn't enough to hide the faint scrape of footsteps on the concrete, and someone moving silently on the dock that separated Rum Runner from Hobo. I figured it was Salisbury, returning with a friend. Then I heard the popping sound of the light bulb at the end of the dock being smashed by something like a towel wrapped around a fist, and that didn't sound right. I reached for my pistol.

More hushed voices. I climbed out of my bunk and stood barefoot and in my boxer shorts as I looked out the porthole in the galley. This is what I told the cops I saw: A slightly-built man with pointy elbows and strong forearms stood on the dock about ten feet from me. A second man, with a beefy build, had climbed aboard Rum Runner. He was momentarily silhouetted against the shrimp boat's lantern as he slipped into the open door of the main cabin. Two shots, fired with a silencer, plucked the still air. They were followed moments later by a third shot.

I climbed the companionway steps and raised my Sig Sauer. "Don't even think about moving."

The man on the dock stiffened as his partner emerged from Rum Runner's cabin.

"Drop your weapon," I said.

But some people don't listen.

I already had a bead on him, and no time to think about it. He fired first, the bullet went wide. I squeezed the trigger. There was a grunt, followed by a splash.

"Demetri!" the skinny man shouted. He looked at me, and then made a break for it. He took off fast, and I didn't chase him. I climbed off Hobo and hopped aboard Rum Runner. Andrew, the first mate, was in his bunk. The sheets were soaked in blood and he was dead. There was no sign of Evan Salisbury.

THREE

Three minutes later the first cops arrived.

The cop with the flashlight took my weapon and bagged it, told me not to touch anything. After a while more cops arrived. Some of them found an inflatable dingy and went to get Demetri, who by now had drifted about twenty feet into the channel. They wore latex gloves. They couldn't lift the dead weight over the side of the boat, so they towed him to the dock, where more policemen dragged his corpse onto a stretcher. Within half-an-hour lights had been set up on the dock so the investigators could look for evidence. It was like a movie set.

I noticed a lady detective standing on the dock talking to some cops. She had a tall, slim frame and was wearing fitted white pants and an aqua colored blazer and looked like she'd gotten dressed in hurry, her short black hair still wet, tucked behind her ears. A gold badge dangled from a chain around her neck, and I could see the butt of an automatic pistol in a shoulder holster under her jacket. She had good legs and a pair of skimpy sandals, no wedding band, and I figured with shoes like those she must be a pretty good shot.

One of the cops pointed in my direction and she came over, looking at me with dark, intelligent looking eyes. "You're Harry McCoy?"

"That's me."

"And you shot this guy?"

"Yep."

"I'm Consuela Esperanza, homicide. You always carry

13

a gun?"

"I keep one on the boat."

She asked me a lot of questions, and I repeated my story. When I was finished she didn't say anything for a moment.

"Where'd you learn to shoot like that?"

"Quantico, Virginia."

"FBI Academy?"

"I was in the bureau for three years before law school, then I went to work for the Manhattan DA."

She looked at my shabby bathrobe and unshaven face. "You don't look like a DA."

I smiled. "Oh yeah? Well, you don't look like a cop." Then she smiled, and it was one of those nice moments, full of possibilities.

That's when a second detective came out of Rum Runner's cabin and climbed onto the dock. He was heavy set and not good at climbing onto docks. He said his name was Bill Muldoon. He looked like he'd gotten dressed in a hurry, too - a white tennis shirt with the MPD logo pulled over a substantial pouch, and a pair of wrinkled khakis. He had his revolver and badge clipped to his belt. I figured him for about forty, forty-two, he had maybe a couple of years on me.

He looked at his partner. "Boat's registered to Evan Salisbury." He waited for his partner to react. "Yeah, you heard me right, that Evan Salisbury. Victim's name is Andrew Bigelow, worked for Salisbury on the boat."

Muldoon looked down at Demetri. He stared at his face for a long time.

"Friend of yours?" Detective Esperanza asked.

"I thought maybe I recognized him," Muldoon replied, he turned to me. "You ever see him before?"

14

I shook my head.

"You were at the murder scene, we'll have to take your fingerprints, I'm sorry about the ink. They'll have some wipes you can use," said Muldoon.

I nodded that I understood.

"We're gonna need to see your permit."

I had anticipated this after the first uniformed officer to arrive had taken my pistol. I had the permit, issued by the City of New York, in my pocket. Muldoon examined it and handed it back.

I looked over at the deck of Rum Runner, Bigelow was being carried out on stretcher, a sheet covering his body.

"You knew him?" asked Detective Esperanza.

"Met him for the first time a few hours ago."

"So what do you make of it?"

"Back in New York we'd call it a hit."

"Funny, in Miami we call it that too."

The police worked the scene for most of the morning. I made myself comfortable in a chair by the pool. I knew the drill. Fourteen years as an assistant DA in New York had taught me. I'd handled nearly fifty homicides, some of them high profile, like the Dr. Ronald Parkinson case. He was an Upper East Side cardiologist who, according to my theory, gave his wife, Danielle, enough muscle relaxant to kill a racehorse so he could spend more time with his girlfriend. It was daily fodder for the tabloids, and should have been an open-and-shut case. But his lawyer was very good, and the jury, I suspected, a little too fond of the room service at the Radisson. Months of work and it ended in a hung jury, not one of my shining moments.

Still, for the most part, justice has a way of being served. Not so on my last case, the one they said put me

15

over the edge. Maybe I'd been too concerned about making a name for myself building a case against Jimmy Picolo, and I'd reached too far, moved too fast.

Picolo was a mobster, guilty of homicide, and we had a witness who was willing to turn state's evidence. I was in charge of the case, only it went bad, and it was my fault, and a young woman named Lucy was dead because of it. After that I took a medical leave of absence, and then I quit. I was offered a cushy job in a big New York law firm doing criminal defense, but then the recession hit, Lehman Brothers, the housing bust, and the job offer was withdrawn. Leave it to a lawyer to find a way out of an employment contract. So suddenly New York was awash with out-of-work lawyers, and I decided to skip town.

That's when I bought *Hobo*. Like me, she was in pretty sore shape, which I didn't know at the time, because I didn't know anything about boats. I spent four months in a boatyard on City Island getting her ready - new engine, new sails, new rudder, new mast. Ended up being a lot of new things, something yacht brokers call T.L.C.

I took a course to learn how to sail. I gave up my apartment and sold or junked everything that didn't fit on the boat. I know they say you should never move to Paradise, but I was drawn by the promise of sun, and the light. Maybe if I could get to Florida I'd be okay, the dark cloud over my head would lift, and anyway, I wasn't moving there, I was just passing through. I left New York in March, I sailed out of the harbor and pointed her south. *Hobo* and I survived squalls, sandbars, a temperamental diesel and a broken corkscrew, but eventually we arrived in Miami.

I was sitting by the pool, watching the morning sun play on the aqua blue ripples in the water, and wondering

16

when the pool bar would open so I could have a Bloody Mary when the two detectives returned to talk to me.

"Mind if we go over a few things?" asked Muldoon.

"Not at all."

Muldoon scraped two deck chairs over to me and they sat down. "We're guessing Salisbury was the target here, make sense?" he asked.

"I don't know what makes sense."

"The kid didn't have a record, we figure he was just in the wrong place at the wrong time. Anything else doesn't add up," said Muldoon.

"So why didn't they just leave him alone? "

"Maybe they thought he was Salisbury. It was dark right? Maybe they screwed up."

"Maybe. So who'd I shoot?"

"We don't know yet. No wallet, no ID. Must have left it in the car, or it fell out of his pocket when he went into the water," said Detective Esperanza. "Whoever he was, we're guessing he was a pro. He used a silencer, all the more reason why it looks like a hired hit, other than that we don't know much."

"Terrific."

"We're hoping Salisbury can shed some light on who they were, and why they came here."

"Have you contacted him?"

She shook her head. "We were hoping you might be able to help us with that."

I sighed. "Until yesterday afternoon I hadn't seen the guy in 20 years. I have no idea where he'd be."

"But you were friends," Muldoon said.

"A long time ago. We moved in different circles."

Muldoon nodded. "He's got a sister, we've already spoken to her, and a wife. He didn't mention where he was going?"

Detective Esperanza was staring at me. She had a fine complexion, short black hair, now dry, and her two collarbones distinct above the neckline of her shirt. But those deep brown soulful eyes showed a level of concern, interest, empathy, something, it was almost like a hypnotist dangling a gold watch in front of me.

"Anything?" asked Muldoon.

"Huh?"

"He didn't mention anything?"

"No."

"He may have gone to ground," said Detective Esperanza. "You said he wanted to avoid the woman he was divorcing? Why would that be?"

"I don't know her, but I can think of a few reasons."

"He didn't confide in you?" asked Muldoon.

"Like I said, before yesterday I hadn't seen him in twenty years."

"Twenty years, huh? And all of a sudden he's moving in next door."

"Must be my magnetic personality."

Muldoon shook his head. "Looks like you really stepped in something. This marina doesn't have security?"

"There's a gate, which is almost always locked. Everyone has a key. And there's a security guard, part time, he pops in every now and then. Of course if they launch an attack from the sea we're defenseless."

"Gate didn't stop what happened last night."

"No, it didn't."

"I'd be concerned about that, if I were you."

"So does that mean I get my weapon back?"

"Sorry. It's evidence." He looked me in the eyes. "You might want to think about relocating."

"You know how hard it is to find an inexpensive slip in Miami? I'm not exactly made of money."

"I'm sure you can figure something out. I just don't want one of Demetri's friends deciding to pay you another visit," said Muldoon.

"I don't remember reading about any of this on the Miami department of tourism website."

"It's a big city, like anyplace else."

Maybe it was the apathy that had descended on me since Lucy died. Maybe I was spoiling for a fight. Whatever it was, the detective's warning didn't alarm me as much as it probably should have.

"Well, I kind of like it here. Don't much feel like moving. No, I think I'll stay put."

"Your decision."

The fact was I was exhausted, and didn't know what I would do.

They stood up. "We're around, call us if you think of anything, and we'll be in touch if any information turns up that we think you should know."

They both gave me their cards. Half an hour later, after the detectives had gone, the security guard showed up. His name was Lopez, I'd never really spoken to him before, other than to say 'hello.' He was surprised to see all the commotion. I saw him getting the full story from Lapidus, who lived on a trawler in the marina. Lopez's mouth hung open in surprise. That made me feel sorry for him. Nothing ever happened at the marina, now something finally had, and he'd been somewhere else. Asleep, probably.

Lopez was dressed the way he always dressed, cotton cargo shorts and a white shirt with epaulets, and cop paraphernalia clipped everywhere.

He came over to me. "Crazy shit, huh?"

"I'll say."

"So who was this guy you shot?"

"Think his name's Demetri, but he's still a John Doe."

"Demetri, I don't like the sound of that."

"Me either." Miami was awash with Russian gangsters, and lately a few had made headlines with their heavy-handed business style.

Lopez asked a bunch of other questions, and I answered as best I could.

"Why all the questions, do you have to file a report?" I asked.

"Report?"

"For Ramsgate?" Ramsgate was the name of the security company.

He picked at his uniform shirt. "I just work for Ramsgate on the side. I also got my own business. Private investigator. I just like to know what's going on, is all."

He took out his wallet and handed me his card. It said his first name was Steven, and he was a licensed P.I. He leaned back on the chaise beside me.

"I went straight into it when I got out of the army."

"M.P.?"

He shook his head.

"Special Forces."

I raised an eyebrow.

"Oh yeah, Iraq, and a few other places, right out of high school. That's what got me interested in this line of work."

He looked at me to see if I understood. "My job description was 'strictly need-to-know,' if you know what I mean." He made quotation marks with his fingers.

"I mean, I could tell you what I did," he had the timing

20

down to a tee, and his delivery was deadpan.

I ruined it for him. "But then you'd have to kill me. Sorry."

His face dropped. "Seriously, we got into some heavy shit. I don't even like to talk about it."

"Okay."

"Maybe once in a while, you know, like over a beer or something like that."

"I understand."

"Yep, I was in some heavy shit, some *heavy* shit."

I wondered if Lopez was for real, Army Special Forces, or if he'd been in the quartermaster corps, stockpiling toilet paper in a US Army warehouse somewhere, all very hush-hush.

FOUR

Around lunchtime I arrived at the home of my Uncle Morris and Aunt Mimi. I was driving a loaner from Uncle Mo. My choice had been a 98 Rabbit convertible or a 2006 white Cadillac. I'd opted for the bunny. The a/c was broken, but it wasn't bad with the top down.

They had just returned from their annual month-long trip away from the summer heat of Miami. I'd been keeping an eye on their place. Mo hated travel, but Mimi insisted. If she wanted to climb an Alp, he climbed an Alp, if she wanted to go to Venice, he hired a gondola. They'd just returned from Italy, and left a message on my cell phone. I'd been living on reheated Chinese food and sandwiches from the local convenience store, so despite how tired I felt, I jumped at the offer of lunch.

"You look like you could use a drink," said Uncle Mo.

I couldn't argue with him. My uncle knew nothing if not how to mix a drink.

"How about a Bloody Mary?"

"One Bloody comin' right up."

We were sitting on the patio of their house overlooking the Intracoastal. It was a high-security island called Coral Cove, off the causeway that linked Miami and Miami Beach. Uncle Mo sported a worn blue linen jacket and beige trousers. In his advancing years, his clothes had become roomy, the trousers pulled up and cinched above his waist so his pale blue socks showed. He had bushy eyebrows and a gray moustache and a small, wiry frame.

"How was your trip?" I asked.

He let out a sigh. "Worst one yet."

"Oh Mo, it wasn't that bad," said Aunt Mimi, stepping through the sliding glass doors onto the patio. She was considerably larger that Uncle Mo.

"The hell it wasn't," said Uncle Mo, who went on to tell me how an Italian taxi driver had tried to overcharge him, and then described the plumbing arrangements in the hotel.

"So how are things with you?" he asked.

"No worse than usual."

"How's the marina working out?" asked Aunt Mimi.

"Pretty good. Had an intruder last night. He killed someone, I shot him."

Uncle Mo nearly gagged on his Bloody Mary. "You what?"

"Tell us everything, and don't leave anything out," insisted Aunt Mimi.

I did as I was told.

"Do you know who this man was, the one who attacked you?" she asked when I was finished.

"Demetri somebody, and he didn't attack me, well he did shoot at me, I suppose that's the same thing. I think he was there to murder someone named Evan Salisbury."

"Whoa, wha?" said Uncle Mo.

"Evan Salisbury, it was his boat. You know him?"

"Sure I know him, or rather I should say I know of him. Did business with his dad."

Uncle Mo was an engineer by training, inventor of something called the Marsh bi-valve, which was used in commercial air conditioners. He'd gotten into ventilation systems right after the Korean War and was responsible for the arctic temperatures in many of Miami's big hotels. As Miami grew, so had his business. Ten years earlier he'd sold out to a national construction firm, leaving him with a pile of dough and not enough to do.

"Like I said, I knew his dad, and his uncle, they ran Salisbury Steel," said Uncle Mo. "Big operation, used to be anyway. They were fabricators, steel buildings, stuff like that, steel shipbuilders, too, if I'm not mistaken. Been around for a hundred years, at least. We used to buy steel from them. Then they got into other things. Real estate mostly. Worth millions. In those days an outfit like that could make good money. Things have changed. That's why they ended up all real estate, I guess they got caught in the bubble."

"Evan runs the business?"

Uncle Mo wiggled his hand. "Never all that interested in the day to day. They hired big guns to run the business. Evan is on the board, I think. The cops think something happened to him?"

"Too soon to say, but looks like he's disappeared."

"Jesus. He's worth big bucks, I can tell you that. Half the high rises in Miami are built with their steel, and Salisbury Real Estate Holdings owns most of them. If you wanted to kidnap someone, I'd say he'd be a good candidate."

After lunch, when we were sitting in the den, Uncle Mo leaned forward and slapped me on the knee.

"Harry, I don't know how to say this so I'm just going to come out and say it."

"Say what?"

"Do you need to talk to someone, you know, a shrink?"

"No, why?"

"Just someone to talk to."

"A therapist, he means," said Aunt Mimi.

"Why would I need that?"

"You just killed a man."

24

"That makes me crazy?"

"We were thinking of post traumatic stress disorder."

"If I start acting nuts you have my permission to have me committed."

Uncle Mo shook his hand. "No, no, no. It's not like that and you know it. And it's not about being crazy. Let's face it, that thing in New York, now this, you've been through a lot."

"Tell you what, if it turns out to be a problem I'll talk to someone."

Uncle Mo searched my face to see if he believed me.

"Okay kid, that's all I'm asking."

He slapped me on the knee again.

"Thanks, Uncle Mo."

FIVE

I returned to the marina later that afternoon. Someone, I assumed it was the police, had collected Rum Runner while I was gone. The air was cooler now, and since I'd been up almost all night, I was planning a siesta. Michaela, the woman from the front office who had rented me the slip, stood in my way.

"May I have a word?"

She had her arms crossed, and was tapping her very pointy shoe. Michaela was in charge of leasing apartments in the adjoining Biscayne Towers, but business was slow, so management made her run the marina too. She wasn't happy about it. As a result, she was a strict enforcer of the rules, which was a shame, since she was otherwise a very attractive woman.

"Would you like a cold drink?" I asked. "A Coke or a beer?"

"No thank you," she said. "I need to talk to you about last night."

"Oh?"

"You know the marina has a strict rule about firearms."

"I didn't know that."

"It's in the agreement you signed."

"I didn't actually read it."

"It says 'no guns.'"

"Then how do we defend ourselves?"

"That's why we have Esteban."

"Who's Esteban?"

"Our guard?"

"Lopez?"

"Yes."

"What if he isn't here?"

"It doesn't matter, you can't have a gun."

"The Second Amendment of the Bill of Rights says I can."

"The Condo Association by-laws say you can't."

"Sounds like a case for the Supreme Court, we'll probably never get to the bottom of it."

She reminded me of my ex-girlfriend, Fiona. I'd dated Fiona for two years. Then everything happened, and Fiona was caught in the middle. A nice girl, really, but now very angry at me. Extremely angry. Furious, really. I remembered when I'd told her I wouldn't be taking the job at the law firm, that I was leaving New York. That hadn't gone over well.

"When you say you're taking a break, just what exactly do you mean?" she'd asked.

"It's time to do something else. I'm taking a break."

"How can you take a break?"

"I was thinking I might buy a sailboat and cruise the Caribbean."

The decision was made as I spoke. I guess I had Fiona to thank for that.

"What do you know about boats?"

"I'll learn."

"I see. And just when exactly is all this happening?"

"I guess it's happening now."

Her arms had been crossed and she was tapping an expensive Bottega Veneta shoe on the parquet floor of her 73rd Street apartment. I knew because she'd dragged me shoe shopping with her, which is about the worst thing a woman can do to a man. That was when I knew she was

27

really steamed that all her efforts to improve me had failed. She would have to cancel a meeting she'd gone to great pains to set up with a partner at a top Wall Street law firm.

Her expression was one of disgust, then contempt. I could practically see the wheels turning as she recalculated who she could get to bring her to the Met Gala, or whatever it was, since it obviously wouldn't be me, and it wouldn't be me in Bridgehampton, either.

Instead I'd found Hobo.

"Are you sure you wouldn't like that drink?" Michaela still had her arms crossed. "I think we're at an impasse."

I found myself attracted to her. Michaela had a willowy frame and blonde hair.

"No. Thank you."

"What do you have against guns, anyway?"

"They're against the rules. Look, I don't mean to be a bitch or anything, but we have insurance, and rules."

"The police took it so the issue's moot."

Her eyes narrowed and she glared at me. "I guess that's fine, just consider yourself warned. I'm going to put this in the file as well."

"Good idea. I think you should."

Truth be told, I also had an M1 Garand rifle under my bunk, the idea being so I could fend off bandits on the high seas, or at least have a fighting chance, if it ever came to that. I didn't tell Michaela about it. People don't need to know everything.

I took a short nap, and when I woke up I strolled around the marina. There was an informal cocktail circuit among the live-aboards, and I found a small gathering aboard Ted Lapidus' trawler.

Ted ran a medical supply business from the yacht, bedpans and wheelchairs, and lived with his wife, Jane.

28

There was also Virginia. She was a friend of Ted and Jane. She was cruising with them, and not what you'd call shy around men.

"To think there were murderers here, right here. And that boy is dead," Virginia said.

"Let's just hope they don't come back, out of revenge or something," said Jane.

"How do you know they won't?" said Frank DeNardis, who lived aboard a 50-foot ketch in the slip next to the Lapiduses and who seemed to eat most of his meals aboard their boat.

"If they come back Lopez will protect us," said Lapidus, removing tobacco from its pouch and tamping it into his pipe. "Anyway, why would they be interested in you?"

"Why would they be interested in anybody? Why were they interested in that poor kid? And who's they?" said Virginia.

"Exactly," I said.

Lapidus touched a match to his pipe and puffed on it until it was lit. He smoked his pipe and nodded his head and no one said anything for a while.

"Have you met the new girl yet?" he asked, resuming the conversation, "her name is Cameron. Cameron." He repeated her name slowly, like it meant something.

"Who?"

"She arrived this afternoon, while you were at lunch. The Hunter 38."

The new arrival had also caught the interest of DeNardis. His ketch was "Lady Luck," which was ironic. He was a bachelor who'd made a killing in bonds or something. He had purchased his boat thinking it would help him meet women. So far, he had confessed to me, its power to attract had disappointed. I wasn't surprised. DeNardis had just showered and reeked of aftershave, which I suspected may have been part of his problem.

"How old is she?" asked DeNardis.

"Thirty, maybe," said Virginia. "There's a story there. I couldn't put my thumb on it."

"Don't start gossip," said Ted.

"Just something curious about her," continued Virginia. "I guess you're right, I shouldn't say anything. It's just, when I talked to her, I had the sense she was running from something."

"Oh Jesus," said Lapidus.

I had a hangover the next morning, not uncommon lately. I was standing on the dock in a bathing suit and flip flops, drinking coffee and hosing off Hobo's deck, a morning ritual, when I met the new arrival myself. She had a blond ponytail pulled through the back of a Florida Marlins baseball cap.

"You must be my new neighbor, I'm Harry."

She gave me and Hobo a quick once over. I wasn't sure she was impressed.

She held out her hand, "Cameron Blake."

"You live aboard the boat?"

"My ex-boyfriend kept the apartment."

Virginia's intuition wasn't far off the mark.

"I heard about you yesterday, so are you a cop or something?" she asked.

"Nope, not anymore. Just a regular person."

"Who happens to sleep with a loaded pistol."

"I don't actually sleep with it."

"So is it quiet at night, when there's no shooting?"

"For the most part. In fact, it'll be nice to have some

company, it's usually too quiet," I replied.

"That's what I want – the quiet, not the company – you know what I mean."

I noticed a small dog in the cockpit of her boat. He was trying to jump onto the dock, taking tentative steps with his short legs, then backing away.

"That's Siegfried," she said. "He's part Yorkshire terrier, part something else."

She whistled and the small dog finally jumped from the stern lazarette to the deck and then onto the dock where he proceeded to sniff my shoe. He was a scruffy little thing, couldn't have been more than ten or twelve pounds. He wandered off down the dock to relieve himself against a potted palm tree. A car horn sounded beyond the marina's gate.

"That'll be my ride," said Cameron.

She put the dog back on the boat, and he obediently disappeared through a small doggie door built into the companionway.

"He stays on the boat?" I asked.

"It's air conditioned. He has his own door, he's fine. And don't worry, he won't bark. See you later."

"I'll be around."

I picked up my newspaper and collected my mail from the front desk and walked down the crushed seashell path to the pool. I installed myself beneath a massive banyan tree that ruled over the southern end of the pool deck.

The paper reported the murder and mentioned my name. Thanks, I thought, that's really helpful. There was a big photo of Salisbury taken at a fancy party. He was laughing, holding a glass of champagne and standing next to beautiful woman who was identified as Christina, his

31

wife. It said that his family had posted a reward. It said they were anxious to find him.

After I'd finished the paper, I peeled myself out of the chair, and did a splashy dive into the deep end of the pool. I did two laps submerged before coming up for air, rolled over and floated on my back in the shallow end for a few minutes, then climbed out and collapsed in the chaise longue.

In theory, a guy could get pretty comfortable here, waiting out storm season, I thought. The truth was I was bored, and worried that if South Florida wasn't doing it for me, what would? It was a lack of purpose that was making me sink deeper into the existential funk that had started back in New York. I hoped my outlook would improve when I headed south again, but I suspected it would not. The question remained, where was I going, and what would I do when I got there?

My plan was to shove off in three or four weeks, when the threat of hurricanes was over. I was going by the book, Van Dorn's *Oceanography and Seamanship*. In the chapter on weather, it said "a mature hurricane is a formidable thermodynamic engine, devoutly to be eschewed."

So there I was, eschewing devoutly, when a woman walked up to me and stopped at the foot of the chaise.

"Are you Harry McCoy?"

I squinted into the sun and told her I was.

"I'm Valerie Shoupe, my brother is Evan Salisbury. I think we actually met, years ago."

If we had I would have remembered. Valerie Shoupe was a petite woman. She had short curly brown hair, brown eyes and sharp features. All in all she was very well formed. She had on shorts and a linen safari jacket with most of the top buttons undone.

I stood up and offered her a seat. "Have you heard from Evan?"

She shook her head.

"Last time I spoke to him was the day before yesterday. He told me he met you, and was moving the boat here, he was always checking in. Normally he lives in my pool house. Well, Dad's pool house. Anyway, he hasn't been home."

"He said his wife threw him out?"

"Something like that. Probably a blessing in disguise."

"Do you think she had anything to do with this?" I asked.

She shook her head. "The police told me what you did. Thank you for trying to help Evan. You seem like a resourceful man, Mr. McCoy."

"Call me Harry."

"And I'm Valerie. I don't know why I came here. I guess to meet you. This is just so crazy, I don't know what to do. Did Evan say anything to you?"

"What do you mean?" I asked.

"It just seems strange, him running into you, then coming here, and then what happened to that poor boy."

I shook my head. "It occurred to me that your brother was running from something. He was in an awfully big hurry to find a place to tie up, strange for a man like your brother, don't you think? I mean, he could go anywhere he wanted. He said he'd been fishing, but I didn't see any fishing tackle on the boat."

"You're very observant."

"He told me he went fishing in the Bahamas, too. I figured he was partying over there."

"Have the police told you anything?"

She shook her head. "No, I've decided to offer a

33

reward, and hire a private investigator."

She looked at me, like a light bulb had just turned on. "You could find him."

I smiled and shook my head, but the idea took hold.

"I could pay you to find him. You've already proven yourself."

"Sorry, I'm a lawyer, not a private detective, and I'm not much of a lawyer these days."

"I bet you're an excellent lawyer. You're certainly not like the lawyers I know. I'm willing to pay whatever the going rate is."

"I wouldn't even know what that is."

"If he's alive I want him back, if he's dead...." She hesitated. "Anyway, the reward is $50,000."

"That's a lot of money, probably more than you need to offer."

"I'm a rich woman, Mr. McCoy – Harry," she looked me squarely in the eyes.

"And you're used to getting what you want?"

"It would be money well spent if it helps me find my brother. He's my only family."

She had slim fingers and wrists with gold bangles and no wedding ring. As I contemplated her offer, she watched my face like a poker player.

"Not that I'm agreeing to help, but just out of curiosity, what's Evan mixed up in?"

"What do you mean?"

"People with guns don't normally show up in the middle of the night to kill you if you aren't mixed up in something."

"I don't know."

"Take a guess."

"Since he left the family business he's been involved in

a lot of business deals. If he handled them in the same cavalier way he handled our family company, I imagine there are people out there who don't like him very much."

"Enough to try to kill him?"

She shrugged.

"What sort of business deals?" I asked.

"So you're interested?"

I shook my head. "Like I said, I'm not your man. If you must know, I'm not in law enforcement anymore. I was for a while, but not now. And don't ask me to explain, it's a long story. If you really want to find your brother, you're better off hiring someone else."

"I'm not so sure. I think you're a man who doesn't play by the rules. I think you're the kind of man I need."

It was hard to say no to a woman like Valerie Shoupe. Miami was an expensive town, and I hadn't allowed for getting held over for storm season. I thought it would be nice to have extra money in hand before I hit the gaming tables and racetracks in the Cayman Islands, so part of me wanted to take her up on the offer. Instead, I told her I'd think about it. She took a card out of her purse and handed it to me.

"Opportunity is knocking, Harry. I suggest you open the door."

SIX

I slipped on the least wrinkled pair of khaki trousers I could find and a tennis shirt, aware that all my clothes were slightly damp and beginning to smell of mildew. Beginning to? Who was I kidding? But they were all I had. After a quick bite at the S & S diner, I headed over to police headquarters. I'd had a call from Detective Muldoon saying they wanted to talk.

Detective Consuela Esperanza had a small office on the third floor of the Miami Police Headquarters. It was located in downtown Miami, on 2nd Avenue, not far from Little Havana. She was sitting behind her desk, finishing a phone call and Muldoon was leaning on the air conditioner. He had a cup of coffee in his hand and looked tired, same as the day before.

Cops' offices always look sparse, undecorated, because good cops spend most of their time on the street. Detective Esperanza's was no exception, except she had a yucca plant, and it looked like she watered it once in a while, too. There was also a framed photo of her standing between two people who I assumed were her father and mother. It looked like it was taken when she graduated from the Police Academy. Her dad was very distinguished looking, in his early seventies. He was wearing a beige suit and sunglasses, and had a dark tan and white hair. Her mother was younger, maybe around sixty, a tall, lean woman with the same healthy complexion as her daughter, and graying hair cut very short. I saw where Detective Esperanza got her looks.

Detective Esperanza hung up the phone. "We tracked down the vic's next of kin. Andrew Bigelow's family live in the Gables. Just graduated from Florida State. Met Salisbury through a sign he posted at Earl's Boatyard, down in South Miami, signed on to help with the boat. His father said he'd been spending all his time with Salisbury, been away days at a time, didn't say doing what."

"Seemed like a good kid," I said.

"We ID'd the shooter, too," added Muldoon. "You're not going to like it. He has a record. Name's Demetri Popov. Member of Juri Epstein's crew here in Miami."

He looked straight at me and raised an eyebrow.

I shrugged. "Should that name mean something to me?"

"Juri Epstein. Russian émigré, possible mob connections. Make that likely mob connections. Started out as a thug, Moscow black market. Now he passes himself off, pretty convincingly I might add, as an international businessman," Muldoon explained.

"And let me guess, we gave him a green card?"

Detective Esperanza spoke. "He's donated about a million bucks to local charities trying to establish himself as legit, plus he's a major political donor. He's a citizen now, too."

"How'd he get all his money?"

"No one seems to know, he has a chain of nightclubs and hotels plus a bunch of other stuff. You ask me, they're cover for something else."

"A great way to launder money."

She nodded. "No inventory, lots of cash."

"So what laws is he breaking?"

She shrugged. "None, that we know of."

She handed me a file. "Here's what we have on the guy

you shot. Demetri Popov."

His photo was stapled to the inside of the file. A mug shot. He was bald, big and strong like a piano mover, and he had the vacant, emotionless look of someone who knows how to pose for a mug shot. Maybe I was reading into it, but I thought he also looked like a man who killed for a living, and didn't think twice about it. His life was just a police file now, thanks to me. Not that he didn't deserve it, but you think about those kinds of things when you look at the face of man you killed.

I leafed through the file.

"I see here he got arrested."

"One charge of felony assault. Bit someone's ear off in a parking lot. Charges were dropped."

"Who drops the charges after their ear is bitten off?" I asked.

"Depends who's doing the biting. It was enough that INS looked into it, figured maybe the work he was doing for the visa wasn't on the up and up. There was an investigation. They pulled some records from Moscow police, not much there, but an outfit called Liberty International named Popov in the murder of a Russian journalist who had been investigating corruption in the government. He had his head blown off. Popov was also linked to the murder of some Russian mining executive. Deportation proceedings were in the works."

"So he's a trigger man."

"There's more," said Muldoon.

"I don't like where this is going."

"He had a cousin, at least we think it's a cousin, name's Vladimir Drestikoff, but everyone calls him Junior."

"Lemme guess, whoever gave him the nickname was being ironic."

Muldoon cleared his throat. "Moved down here last year from your neck of the woods, Far Rockaway. Our informant said he wants you dead."

"Wonderful."

"So far, we can't locate him, but word on the street is he's offering ten grand," he said.

"That's embarrassing, but it should keep the real pros away, you know, snipers from Detroit and such." I was trying to stay cool. I didn't want Muldoon to see my Adam's apple move.

"It also means you could have half the thugs in Miami out gunning for you, anyone who wants to make a quick buck. Times are tough," said Detective Esperanza.

I breathed deeply and looked back at Popov's file. Popov was an enforcer, and in Russia guys like that had plenty of work. Given that he didn't look particularly intelligent, I assumed brutality ranked high in his skill set. But I wondered why he'd gone after Salisbury.

"Why'd Popov come to Miami?" I asked.

"Probably got squeezed out, decided to look for new turf. Epstein played a part. We figure the two knew each other in Russia because Epstein sponsored him. We figure he was on Epstein's payroll."

"Doing what?"

"Whatever had to be done," said Muldoon.

Muldoon looked at Detective Esperanza, who pursed her lips. She was leaning against her desk, wearing a hot pink jacket and mint colored skirt. I tried not to stare at her legs.

"We're checking on Epstein," she said. "We want to question him, obviously. We think he's in the Bahamas, where he has business interests, moves around a lot. You should go somewhere, anywhere."

I raised my eyebrows.

"That a problem?" asked Muldoon.

"Valerie Shoupe has asked me to help locate her brother. I told her I'd think about it."

"So tell her you changed your mind," said Detective Esperanza.

Muldoon shifted in his chair. "Kind of out of your jurisdiction, isn't it?"

"I suppose."

He glanced back at his partner. "What kind of caseload did you have up there, in the DA's office? Securities fraud, white collar crime?

"Mostly, other stuff too," I said.

"Well, these guys carry guns," he said.

I ignored the warning. "What are the chances of locating this Junior guy sometime soon?"

Muldoon shook his head. "We're working on it, nothing yet."

He passed me a stack of photos. "These are people who are known to operate in the same circles as Demetri Popov and Juri Epstein, one of them might be the other trigger man."

I looked through them, none of them looked familiar, but leafing through the photos was somewhat intimidating. I tossed them back on the desk. "Anything else to go on?"

"We have sources, something'll break. Meanwhile, you have a problem. Until we know what's going on, be careful. Try to stick with other people, avoid putting yourself in vulnerable positions. You have a license to carry?"

I nodded.

"Might not be a bad idea," said Muldoon.

"That mean I get my gun back?"

"Not yet."

40

"How am I supposed to carry a concealed weapon dressed like this, anyway?" I gestured to what I was wearing, cargo shorts and a tennis shirt. "What do you guys do down here? Don't tell me I have to wear one of those police windbreakers."

"Buy a Hawaiian shirt, or a guayabera," said Detective Esperanza.

"What's that?"

"A Cuban shirt. You don't tuck them in, they cover the gun, it's gotta be concealed," said Muldoon. "Carry the weapon in your belt, behind you, like I do." He raised his arms and did a 360.

"Have you ever considered male modeling?"

For the first time Muldoon cracked a smile.

"Guess I'm going shopping. Before I go, anything turn up on Salisbury?" I asked.

Muldoon shook his head. "He's either dead or he's gone to ground, obviously he's spooked, and for whatever reason, he doesn't want to come to the police. Apparently he's an eccentric character, so I guess that fits. If he is alive, we want to bring him in and figure out what the hell's going on before someone else finds him. But my guess is he's dead."

"Any theories as to why would someone put a hit out on him?"

Muldoon shrugged. "Like I said before, I guess you don't get that rich without making a few enemies along the way."

41

SEVEN

Midday and the marina was dead quiet. Those live-aboards who had jobs, and a surprising number of them did, had ambled off, leaving me feeling like a schoolboy home sick. Alone.

I cleaned Hobo's small wooden cabin, there were lots of nooks and crannies and it was hard to dust everywhere, and after that I pulled together some dirty laundry and carried it to the washing machines in the basement of Biscayne Towers. I returned to Hobo ten minutes later.

I found Virginia wearing a bikini and barefoot. She was reclined on my bunk, her long slender legs stretched out.

"Ted and Jane took the bus to the supermarket. I'm so bored."

"Hi Virginia."

"It's so dull around here during the day."

Virginia rubbed her foot against her tanned calf. She was wearing pink toenail polish.

"You met Cameron?" she asked.

"Cameron?"

"The new girl?"

"Oh yes. Now I remember, I did."

"Did you like her?"

"What's not to like? Ginger ale?"

She ignored the offer. I busied myself pouring one.

"Seemed nice enough," she said. "That's the thing about living on a sailboat, you meet lots of interesting people."

"I'll say."

She sat up on her elbows. The pose was well calculated, and effective.

"You don't mind that I let myself in, do you?"

"No, that's okay."

Now she was up, like a jungle cat, deciding the moment was right to close in.

"You don't sound so sure." She stood in the galley with me, wrapping her arms around my waist. It was getting very warm. My mind was caught off balance by her pheromones. Then rational thought regained a foothold. I gently peeled her arms off. She had a playful look on her face.

"I have an appointment," I said.

"When?"

"Soon."

"How soon?"

"Pretty soon."

"Rats," she said, with a pouting lower lip.

"And I'm not so sure this is a good idea, despite the fact that you're an extremely attractive woman."

She pressed her body against mine.

"Why not?"

"Because it's the middle of the day, and I have work."

"Don't be such a bore."

"Don't take this the wrong way, but I'm under a lot of stress right now, and this is actually making it worse."

"What do you mean?"

"This whole Russian assassin thing has really thrown me for a loop."

"Poor baby. You are tense," and she pulled me onto the bunk and started giving me a massage.

Two hours later I was at my gym in Coconut Grove.

43

Javier, the resident trainer, could be tough when I hadn't been in for a few days, which I hadn't. He faked a punch and then gave me two in the arm for flinching. He thought it was very funny. Luckily the family DNA was pretty good, and I wasn't one of those people who spends their life on the treadmill. I did have a little flab around the mid section, I'll admit, but I wasn't too worried about it. I figured I could draw off it if I ever got shipwrecked.

Javier put me through a punishing routine on weights and then made me climb the stairs to the roof and do fifty push-ups and two sets of lunges. I finished the workout with twenty minutes on the bike machine while I watched the news on a TV mounted on the wall.

To the staccato beat of the station's theme music, slick graphics dissolved to an image of the marina. They teased the story before going to a commercial: "Is a murderer on the prowl on the Miami waterfront? Neighbors want to know, and police are seeking answers." They played up the missing millionaire angle. This time they didn't give my name, but they named the marina, which anyone could recognize, and showed a video of Lopez waving off the camera. Why not just paint a target on my head, I wondered.

When I returned to Hobo, Virginia was nowhere to be seen. I showered and changed and decided not to stick around. There was a Nicaraguan eatery I liked called La Barca de Pescadora, which I think means fishing boat, on Calle Ocho. They served a lunch special of black beans, rice and fried plantains for $3.99. I had more than a few beers, too, since it was about 95 degrees out and they went down like water. It wasn't like I had anything else planned. I was feeling no pain on the way home, and did a pretty lousy parking job on the cul-de-sac near Biscayne Towers.

In Miami the vinyl upholstery of a car sticks to your skin like hot glue, so I used a windshield sunshade on the dashboard. It helped a little. I reached into the car to put it in place, unfolding it along its creases. The early afternoon sun hit the tin foil surface and reflected onto a car across the street. That's when I noticed the white Chevy Suburban with tinted windows. The engine was running, the windows were closed. Through the tinted windows I could see a man in the front seat.

I didn't like the look of it. I tossed the cardboard into the car and as I closed the door I heard a loud pop, and a bullet hole appeared in my windshield. The glass spider-webbed. It was the only sign I needed. I turned and ran as fast as I could. I was sober now, but maybe not sprinting as fast as I normally could. Out of the corner of my eye, I caught sight of a man wearing dark glasses. He was running diagonally across the street toward me. My foot hit the curb and I tripped, sprawling on the sidewalk. My legs felt rubbery and my heart was beating faster than I could remember. The gunman was just a few feet away. He raised his pistol.

"This is for Demetri," he said.

I heard a shot.

The first bullet hit him in the chest, it was followed almost immediately by a second in the side of the head. The kill shot. Blood splattered on the sidewalk. The gunman collapsed on the pavement. I looked up the block. There was Lopez, in a crouch position, both hands gripping his pistol.

EIGHT

My would-be assassin was a two-bit hood with a rap sheet that included burglary, armed robbery, and drug possession. His name was Emmanuel Rivera. Muldoon said he would be the first of many. The detective was starting to grow on me. He was a glass-half-empty person, like me. Maybe one day we could have a discussion on West Nile Virus, or electro-magnetic pulse bombs. Again, he suggested I split town, instead I decided to pay a visit to Valerie Shoupe.

She lived on Old Cutler Road in the fancy part of Coconut Grove. A substantial cement wall surrounded the house, a wall designed not to impress, but to keep people out. It must have been nine feet tall, with red roofing tiles which formed a peak on top, and broken glass on top of that. I announced myself over an intercom at the wrought iron gate, which slowly rolled open, revealing a sprawling two-story house on an immaculate and well-watered lawn.

Valerie Shoupe greeted me on the front steps and led me across a large marble floored foyer to the living room. The house wasn't decorated, it was curated. The walls were hung with paintings ranging from modern to 17th century Dutch, the furniture looked like museum pieces, too.

"Do you mind if I smoke? I'm one of the last people I know who hasn't kicked the habit," she asked as we sat down.

"Not at all."

She put a cigarette in her mouth and tried to light it

with a lighter that was set into a large crystal cube. "You've decided to take the case?"

"I'd like to help you if I can, still not sure I'm the best man for the job."

The lighter wouldn't work, I think it was the flint, so she put the cigarette down. She looked right at me and dropped her voice. She had the voice drop down to a tee.

"You're making the right decision. Business first. How much does a man like you charge?"

"Well, I guess my rate would five hundred bucks a day. Plus expenses." I quoted that number because it was the first number that popped into my head, and added the "plus expenses" as an afterthought, because I'd always heard Rockford say that on TV. I didn't know how much private investigators charged, but I figured it was more than I'd made on the Investigative Division of the Manhattan DA's office.

We shook hands. She held onto my hand, and locked eyes. "Done," she said.

"You mentioned before that your brother invested in business ventures. I got the idea you didn't think much of them."

"Salvage projects, a very expensive hobby, Mr. McCoy – Harry – not an investment."

"Who else was involved?"

She shrugged her shoulders. "I'm not sure. Our business manager could probably tell you. There were more than a few partners who had Evan figured for a patsy. Let me show you."

Valerie led me to the back door, down a limestone path that ended at a keystone patio overlooking the bay. A pair of bronze cannons guarded the approach. Though it seemed impossible, the property was actually more

47

impressive from the water side than from the street. It must have looked great from the deck of a robber baron's yacht. The immense lawn was punctuated with statues of Greek gods, the largest of which was a very Baroque Poseidon, presiding over Biscayne Bay.

"My great-grandfather built it," she said. "Now we're the ones who have to struggle to keep it up. If it were any bigger we'd have had to sell it years ago."

"I'd hate to be the guy who has to mow the lawn."

She smiled. "Don't think I haven't considered getting a herd of goats, or sheep or whatever, but who wants all the goat shit. We divided the property, that helped. That's the guesthouse, Evan moved there a few months ago, for the divorce."

"I'd like to poke around in there, if that's okay."

We walked across the grass.

She tilted her head to one side and smiled. "You don't remember me, do you?"

My expression indicated I did not.

"It was a long time ago. I visited Evan in college. Stayed in his room, in a sleeping bag."

"Come to think of it, I do remember something."

"Liar," she smiled. "But I remember you. You always remember the people ahead of you in school, not the younger ones. You lived down the hall from Evan, and you played soccer."

"You have a good memory."

"I remember certain things."

We arrived at the guesthouse. It was a white tropical-looking bungalow, I guess you might call the style Caribbean colonial, with French doors facing the glittering blue swimming pool. There was a pool man in a pith helmet fishing a leaf out of the water. She swung open the door and drew a sharp breath.

The place had been tossed.

Evan's digs consisted of a large airy living room, a kitchenette, bedroom, and bath. It was expensively decorated with white upholstery, rich beige carpeting and dark wood floors, tasteful art on the walls. But drawers were overturned, clothes and possessions scattered on the carpet. Someone had gone though the place in a hurry.

"When was the last time you were here?"

"Right after the shooting. I was looking for Evan."

"And everything was in order then?"

"Yes, the only thing I remember noticing was that his gold mini was missing from the driveway."

"He drove a mini?"

She nodded.

"I'll need the license number. So he never left it like this?"

"Never."

"I'm going to have to come back later to do a thorough search, but for now we should have the police dust for prints, not that I think they'll find any. Any idea how someone would gain entry into the house?"

"Climb over the wall, I guess, or by boat. We have a houseboy who's supposed to keep an eye on things, but he does the grocery shopping for several hours every day, and he has most evenings off." She crossed her arms tightly. "What has Evan gotten himself into?"

"You tell me."

I made the call and 20 minutes later two patrol officers arrived, and a few minutes after that Muldoon showed up with a CSI guy to dust for prints. Valerie and I sat down in deck chairs by the pool.

"I need to know everything," I said. "The good, the

49

bad, the ugly."

"Like what?"

"For starters, what kind of people is Evan mixed up with? Does he have a girlfriend, does he take drugs?"

"Evan? No. There is a girlfriend, Regina Chesny, owns a spa in Coral Gables." She spelled it and I wrote it down. "And he had a partner, an Englishman named Bernie Leach, but he's not around anymore."

"What was he like?"

She paused. "He was all right."

"Did they get along?"

"I think so."

"What about you?" I asked. "How do you get along with your brother?"

"We get along just fine."

"When was the last time you spoke with him?"

"Like I said, when he called, the day before he disappeared."

"And when was the last time you actually saw him, face to face?"

"A few days ago, at our lawyer's office. We had papers to sign."

"Did he say or do anything to suggest something was wrong?"

She shook her head.

"What about his family?"

"A wife, if that's what you mean. No kids."

"I'll need to interview her, too."

"Christina, she hangs out at the pool all day, Palm Key Yacht Club."

I made a note of it.

"Tell me about Evan's position in the family business."

She took a deep breath.

"It's mainly a holding company for real estate now. Evan was less involved than he used to be. I don't know much about it."

"Is there anyone who might be able to tell me more about your brother's business affairs?"

"Try Michael Arnett, he handles the day to day affairs at the company. I'll put a call in to him. Salisbury Holdings, Biscayne Boulevard, it's in the book. Anyway, over the last few years, I guess Evan got tired of the company, started getting involved in odd little enterprises."

"Like what?" I asked.

She smiled and rolled her eyes. "Expeditions."

"What kind of expeditions?"

"Evan wanted to be like the guy who found the Titanic. Funded all these expeditions, but no Titanic. Titanic expenses, is all."

"Could you be more specific?"

"Let's see, first there was a British liner that sank in the North Sea back in the 1800's, it was supposed to have gold for the troops in the Crimea. That adventure wasn't exactly what you'd call profitable, but it whet his appetite. Then he spent half a year off Nantucket looking for some steamship that went down during the Civil War, supposed to have gold on that one too. Evan had gold on the brain. Spent hundreds of thousands and all he found were lumps of coal. Then there was the Guadeloupe. Jesus, what a bust. He rented a big ship, a crew, a video production company. It even had a submersible. Submersibles are very expensive, Harry."

"I bet."

"You know what he found?"

I shook my head.

"A bunch of old bottles mostly. No gold, no silver."

"Was he involved in a project like that at the time of his disappearance?"

"I sure hope not."

"Anyone I can talk to who might know?"

She shook her head. "He kept things to himself. I guess it goes with the territory. I myself never saw anything in it. It's like those men walking up and down the beach with a metal detector looking for rusty old watches in the sand. That'll probably be Evan when he's older." She stopped short, a look of sadness came over her. A tear rolled down her cheek. She wiped it with her fingers. I patted her on the back.

"I'm sorry," she said. "Anyway, you may as well see it."

She led me behind the guesthouse where stone steps descended to a boathouse. It was like an underground grotto, its keystone arches blackened with age. Here, small boats could be tied up out of the sun. There was room for a larger boat on the dock that jutted out from the boathouse.

"This," she said with a grand sweeping gesture toward a row of heavy steel shelves against one wall, "is what Evan has been doing. You're more than welcome to have a look."

Some of the shelves supported old timbers that must have been salvaged from a shipwreck. There was an anchor, badly rusted and covered in coral, and dozens of glass bottles, very old ones with rounded bottoms, some were sealed shut and some still full of liquid. Most were heavily encrusted, some surprisingly clean. There were hundreds of old cannon balls and cardboard boxes filled with broken crockery.

"He could have kept his boat here," I said. "Why didn't he?"

"He used to, then a few weeks ago he moved it. I figured he was having work done."

"So he wasn't trying to avoid his wife?"

"Why would he have to?"

"Isn't he getting a divorce?"

"Just like everybody else."

I looked around, trying to make sense of it. Salisbury could have tied up here, yet he chose to stay at my marina, which indicated he was definitely on the run. I closed my notebook.

"I think that's all I need, for the time being," I said.

Muldoon was waiting when we got back to the guesthouse.

"We're just wrapping up. You were right, signs point to breaking and entering. Looks like they jimmied the bedroom window in the back," he said.

We followed him through the guesthouse and he showed us the window where a pry bar had gouged the wood around the lock.

"Any idea what they were after?" he asked.

"I'll check, but as far as I can tell I can't see that anything's missing," replied Valerie.

"Meanwhile, we'll run the prints, see if anything interesting turns up," said Muldoon.

Valerie walked us out, back across the lawn, and through the house. She pulled a plastic disposable lighter from her pocket and tried to light another cigarette. The disposable lighter was running out of fluid and wouldn't light. We said goodbye to Muldoon in the driveway, then Valerie walked me to my car where I helped her with the lighter until we got a flame.

"Another nail in the coffin. I'll have to give these up one of these days. My husband couldn't stand it, but then he doesn't have to worry about it any more."

"Divorced?"

"He died."

"I'm sorry."

"Don't be."

As I passed through the front gate under a clouding sky, I looked through the rear view mirror. Valerie was still standing on the front steps of the house, smoking her cigarette, watching me drive away.

NINE

That evening I almost had fish for dinner. A boy fishing from the dock had caught a red snapper, and I tried to cook it on the grill mounted to the stern rail. The filet caught fire, and I ended up throwing the whole thing out and going to a steakhouse on Brickell Key.

To say it had been an eventful day was an understatement. I'd escaped death by the slimmest of margins, and made a career decision. I'd taken on a client. I was in over my head, that was a given. While I was still at the restaurant I found Lopez's card and dialed his number, told him I was looking for help. He agreed to meet me the next morning.

Later that night, I lay in my bunk turning things over in my mind. Valerie Shoupe hadn't even asked why I changed my mind. Maybe people like her were used to getting what they wanted. But that left another riddle. Why had I agreed to take the case? I didn't know Valerie Shoupe from Adam, or Eve, I didn't even know her brother that well, at least not well enough that I owed him. I could use the money, sure, but I could just as easily get along without it. If I still had my shrink, Dr. Sheinborn, he would have wanted to know. He would have wanted me to know. I lay in my bunk as the boat rocked in the gentle waves, and the briny smell of seawater filled my nose, and considered this. Maybe I wanted to be of service to a beautiful woman. Was it really that simple? No. But I was tired, and that was good enough for now.

The next morning I woke to find Hobo blanketed in fog. I dressed quickly in a wrinkled pair of gym shorts and T-shirt and went to buy a newspaper at the newsstand in the lobby. I returned to the cabin, reheated a cup of instant coffee and sat at the table. Something was wrong with the coffee. It was bitter and tasted like... dish soap? I spat it out in the sink and sat down to read the paper, sans coffee. A chart on the front page showed the current mid-Atlantic storms. There was the usual advice on what to do in the event of a hurricane, and I read that home centers were stocking up on plywood and batteries, supermarkets on bottled water, just in case.

I finished my breakfast of a cold bagel with peanut butter and jelly and walked through the underground parking beneath the Towers. After the shooting, I'd decided it was safer to park there, even if it meant paying 30 bucks a day. There was an added advantage, too. The car wasn't broiling in the sun. Someone had placed a flyer under the windshield wiper, which I grabbed before getting in. Only it wasn't a flyer, it was a piece of paper ripped from a notebook.

In handwritten block letters, it read. "Sorry we missed you yesterday. We'll try to connect again soon. Next time you won't be so lucky."

Ten minutes later I met Lopez as arranged. He was wearing a tracksuit and dark glasses and was leaning against the fence surrounding the marina at Bayside Park, watching the Port of Miami.

"Talk to me," he said, as he looked out at the water.

"I want to thank you again for being Johnny-on-the-spot yesterday."

"You're welcome."

"That's not all," I added.

"Oh?"

"I need someone to help me find Evan Salisbury. A man I can trust, someone who knows how to use a gun, someone who knows his way around Miami. A PI license wouldn't hurt."

"Won't find a person like that on Monster.com."

"No, I won't. I should add that the man who killed Andrew Bigelow had ties to Russian gangsters."

"Russians?"

"The guy I shot was named Demetri Popov. Police haven't identified his partner."

"Uh huh."

"Demetri worked for a guy named Juri Epstein, big shot here in town." .

"I think I've heard of him."

"And then apparently Demetri had a cousin, Junior, who's put a contract out on me."

"A contract?"

I nodded.

"Guy tried to kill you yesterday wasn't Russian."

"No, which suggests it's an open contract."

"That's bad," said Lopez.

"Yes."

"Whatever I can do to help. I'm in."

"Don't you want to know how much it pays?"

"Okay, how much?"

"$250 a day, which is half of what I'm charging, plus an even share of the $50,000 reward."

"If we find him alive?"

I nodded.

"Seems like a big reward to find a guy who might just be lying low for a while."

"Could be easy money. But I don't think it will be."

"So when do I start?" he asked.

"How 'bout now?"

Lopez nodded.

"I have a few things to do this afternoon. Maybe you could check your contacts, find out how we can locate a guy named Bernard Leach, and find out as much as you can about him, he was Salisbury's business partner."

"Bernie Leach, got it."

"We'll try to see him tomorrow."

"I'll see what I can do," Lopez said. He hesitated, quietly watching a water taxi clipping through the harbor.

"What's on your mind?" I asked.

"Why'd this lady pick you? Lots of good PIs in Miami."

"I think she trusts me."

Lopez turned and looked at me. "You trust her?"

"She seems alright."

"She telling you everything?"

"Probably not, but her money's good."

"Lot of question marks," said Lopez.

I nodded.

"And you've got a lot of trouble."

"Yes."

"So you think he's still alive?"

"I don't know," I answered.

"So my job's also to watch your back?"

"I'm not sure I need a bodyguard."

"I am." He pointed his finger at me. "And you need a piece. You got a license to carry?"

"I do, but the police haven't given me back my pistol."

He shook his head. "I got a Glock in the trunk, I can let you use it."

I followed Lopez as we walked to his car in the Bayside

58

Mall garage. "Missing person case, I usually start by tracing the subject's last movements before he disappeared, work backwards," he said.

"Sounds like a plan. It would help if we could put the word out on the street. Do you have any good sources?"

"I know a few guys."

His ride was a metallic blue Camaro, an old one, with white vinyl seats and a canvas top that had seen better days, but it looked like he'd done work to enhance the car's performance. There was a chrome exhaust pipe, mag wheels and an air scoop.

He unlocked the trunk and handed me the Glock.

"I'd ask if you know how to use it, but I know you do. Carry it with you wherever you go. Miami can be a dangerous town."

"You're the second person who's told me that."

"You got a shoulder holster?"

I shook my head.

"We gotta get you fixed up."

Lopez said he knew a store called Gun Heaven on Bird Road, where he said I could get anything and everything I wanted. On the way there he said he needed to make a quick stop at his house. He led the way in the Camaro, I followed in the Rabbit, sometimes having trouble keeping up.

Lopez lived in an apartment above his parents' garage in a modest but well kept neighborhood just off Coral Way. There was a cement Virgin Mary in the small front yard surrounded by well-tended marigolds. I waited in the driveway while he went into his apartment. He came out 30 seconds later holding something.

"That what I think it is?" I asked.

"You better take it."

He handed me a bulletproof vest. It was white with Velcro straps.

"You wear this?"

"Me? No," he answered.

"So why do you have it?"

"Well, sometimes I use it, but I think you might need it more. No one has a contract out on me that I know of. Take it, wear it."

Half an hour later we arrived at Gun Heaven. Behind the counter they had enough weaponry to supply an infantry regiment. I was fitted with a leather shoulder holster for the Glock. Then I slipped in the pistol. It had been a while since I wore one.

It felt good.

Then I noticed a nice little Ruger sub-compact, on sale. It was an impulse purchase I couldn't pass up, along with a Velcro holster that fit nicely in the back of my belt, and a pocket holster. Figured they might come in handy.

After that we went to the closest mall and I purchased a lightweight safari jacket and also a tracksuit similar to the one Lopez wore. I tried them on over the vest and shoulder holster. I thought I looked ridiculous, and it was hot and uncomfortable, but Lopez insisted.

It was enough shopping for one day. Lopez had other plans for the afternoon, so I drove north to the Miami Body Salon, the spa owned by Salisbury's girlfriend, Regina Chesny. I carried the Ruger sub-compact in my pocket, it was too hot for the tracksuit, or the vest. The salon occupied a modern concrete and glass building on Miracle Mile in downtown Coral Gables. A tall thin woman with red hair sat at the front desk talking on the phone and leafing back and forth through an appointment book, trying to find an opening.   I figured it was one of those places ladies go to have black stuff put on their faces and lie in tubs filled with hot mud.   I picked up a pamphlet off the desk. It described the benefits of regular colonic irrigation. Treatments started at $80, but if you really wanted to splurge, there was a "total treatment," whatever that was, for $150.

"Lemme guess, you're here for beginning yoga?" the receptionist asked. She was nibbling on the end of her pencil.

I smiled. "Guess again."

"Massage?"

"Nope."

"Men's Pilates?"

"Are you teaching it?"

"Uh uh."

"Then no."

"I give up."

"I'm here to see Regina. Is she around?"

She wrinkled her brow. "I don't know, is she expecting you?"

"No, but if you tell her it's Harry McCoy, a friend of Evan's, she might see me."

The receptionist got up from her desk and indicated with her finger that I should follow. I did. She had a great walk. We went up a flight of steel stairs.

"What's your name?" I asked.

"Cynthia."

"What goes on around here, anyway, Cynthia?"

"People come to get cleansed."

"Easier said than done."

"Tell me about it."

Cynthia showed me to a large exercise room where a

61

dozen or so women in leotards were sprawled on large rubber bouncy balls. It looked like fun, though I didn't see any men in the class, so I probably wouldn't have fit in. She asked me to wait while she told Regina I was there. The woman leading the class was in her mid-thirties, athletic and toned, with the alert look of a successful businesswoman. She had brown hair pulled back in a ponytail, and wore the same black t-shirt that all employees wore. She passed the class off to a pupil and followed the receptionist back to me.

Cynthia smiled. "It was nice to meet you, maybe I'll see you around."

I smiled back. "Maybe."

Regina shook my hand, a curious expression on her face.

"Harry McCoy, a friend of Evan's."

"Has anyone heard anything?" she asked.

"I was going to ask you the very same question."

Her shoulders dropped. "I haven't seen him in over a week. You say you're a friend of his?"

"And I've been hired by his sister to find him."

"Valerie?"

"You sound surprised."

"No, not at all. They're not a close family, that's all, and she's, well, whatever."

"She did take him in when he left his wife."

"That's true"

"And she hired me."

"How thoughtful of her. Let's go somewhere where we can talk."

I followed her past the exercise room to a large terrace overlooking the parking lot behind the building. It was furnished with potted palm trees, teak chairs and oversized umbrellas. There was a bar with a bartender dispensing fruit juice and water. We sat down and the bartender brought us sparkling water.

"I called the police when I heard about the shooting. Spoke to a detective, a woman, she wouldn't tell me anything."

I nodded, "Consuela Esperanza. That's probably because nobody knows anything yet."

"If everything was okay, Evan would have called me. He would have called."

"That's what I was afraid of."

"You think he's dead?"

"I'm not going to lie to you. It's a possibility."

"But not for sure?"

"He could be in hiding, and not want to tell anyone. Or he could have gone away somewhere because he wants people to think he's dead. It's crazy, but who knows. Maybe he's afraid someone might be listening in, so he can't call."

"Or he could be dead. Isn't that more likely? Or kidnapped."

"There hasn't been a ransom note."

"Which means he's probably dead." Another glass-half-empty sort.

"Why are you so sure something bad happened?" I asked.

"Isn't it obvious? We were supposed to have dinner. Of course, he never showed."

"Did he ever miss a date before?"

"Never."

That was a bad sign, especially considering that Regina Chesny was a stand-out in a city filled with beautiful women.

"So what do you think he may have been mixed up with?" I asked.

"His own sister was threatening to sue him, you know. Did she tell you that? They lived a hundred yards apart and she was suing him."

"She didn't mention that."

"I bet she didn't."

"Sue him over what?"

"The business, what else? Complicated stuff, all wills and lawyers and trusts."

"Business is business."

"What does that mean?"

I shrugged. "What do you know about his personal financial situation?"

She wiped her nose. "At the end of the day, despite everything, Evan always seems to have plenty of dough, tons of it by my standards. Granted he made some bad investments, whoo boy, very bad, but there was still plenty left over, trust me. His dad and granddad made it, you know, he was spending it. But there's lots to spend. That's why he attracts all those brilliant partners."

She looked out on the parking lot. The sun was on its way down, and the air was cooling, if only just a little.

"What do you know about these partners?"

"There was one guy, Leach, I met him a couple of times."

"Bernard Leach?"

She nodded. "You know him?"

I shook my head.

"Evan worked with him for a while, thought he was very good, they were going to produce a reality show together, 'Treasure Hunters Miami,' or something like that. I guess it kind of fizzled out. He's a Brit. I always thought

64

he was a con man, myself, at least he comes off that way, real smooth talker, Cockney."

"His sister said he wasn't around anymore."

"I wouldn't know."

"When was the last time you saw him?"

"A couple months ago. Drinks at Evan's place. His sister was there too, in fact."

"Any idea where I can find him?"

Regina shook her head. "I have no idea. Evan doesn't share much about his business."

"Any other business associates that come to mind?"

She thought for a moment. "There was someone. He actually worked for Evan. He had a funny name." She bit her lip while she thought. "Mink, that's it. Clifford Mink. An odd person, worked on the boat, he might know something."

"You have a good memory. Do you know where I can find him?"

"Try the boatyard, Earl what's-his-name," she suggested.

"Earl's Boatyard?"

"That's right."

I knew the place. Muldoon had mentioned it. It was where Andrew Bigelow had signed on to crew for Salisbury. I took a sip of my water and thought about it.

"Can you tell me about the last time you saw Evan? Any little thing could mean something."

"Like I said, that was over a week ago. He used to go away without calling, be gone for a few weeks with hardly a phone call, then show up out of the blue bearing gifts. It wears thin after a while, know what I mean?"

"What happened last week?"

"It was another great date. He drove me out to the

65

Everglades, some godforsaken place in the middle of nowhere."

"Why the Everglades?"

"A meeting with some contractors, some building he was working on. Then he tried to make up for it by taking me to some crummy restaurant at the casino at the Indian reservation out there."

"He's developing land in the Everglades?"

"This was for his own personal use. He wouldn't tell me what it was for. Anyway, he lost a lot of money at the casino," she laughed. "That was the last time I saw him."

She let the full meaning of this sink in. "I hope you find him. Despite his flaws, maybe because of them, I really like Evan."

TEN

Evan Salisbury's wife, Christina Salisbury, was sunning herself at the pool of the Palm Key Yacht Club. Her figure was as near to perfection as was humanly, or divinely, possible. She was wearing a black bikini and at first glance my opinion of Evan Salisbury improved considerably. Maybe he was just a whole lot richer than I thought. Christina was lying on her front, her knee bent, one foot twisting in the air as she leafed through a glossy ladies' magazine.

"Christina?"

She turned and looked at me, momentarily lifting her sunglasses. She looked about ten years younger than Evan, which would put her at about 30. She had short black hair and brown eyes that appeared to be good at sizing people up.

"My name is Harry McCoy. I'm a friend of your husband."

What might have passed for a smile disappeared.

"You're blocking my sun. D'ya mind?"

I stepped to the side, not that she needed any sun. She already had a perfect tan, the color of dark honey, any more and she would overdo it. Maybe she wasn't there for the sun. Maybe she was just resting between laps, not that she needed those, either, there wasn't an ounce of fat on her body.

"I wondered if you'd seen him recently?" I asked.

"I'm sorry, you're who?"

"Harry McCoy, I'm a lawyer. I've been hired to locate

your husband."

"What happened to 'I'm a friend of his?'"

"I'm that too."

"Is this something legal? Does he owe someone money or something?" She turned on her back and sat up on her elbows.

I sat in the chair next to her.

"Nothing like that. I've been retained by his sister, Valerie Shoupe. She's concerned for his safety, which is understandable, seeing as someone tried to kill him Sunday night."

Now the glasses were off and she was lying flat on her back with her eyes closed. She let out a breath.

"I read the papers. So you're a detective, not a lawyer."

"Aren't you concerned about Evan?"

"Sure I'm concerned, but what can I do? I don't even know what it's all about. What is it all about, anyway?"

"That's what I came here to ask you."

"I'd help you if I could, but we don't talk anymore, so I can't. When we meet it's in his creepy lawyer's office, no offense. We're due in court next month, and all I can say is he better be there."

She looked down at her tummy, and then rubbed her hand on it as if somehow that would make it more perfect.

"What if he doesn't show up?"

"Then I guess I don't get my divorce."

The prospect of an early widowhood didn't seem to bother her.

"How long have you been married?" I asked.

"About five years."

"How'd you meet?"

She sighed. "We met when I was a grad student."

"Here in Miami?"

She nodded.

"I was getting my masters in education."

"You're a teacher?"

She shook her head. "No." Stupid question. She folded her fingers and checked her nails, then unfolded them and turned her hand and looked approvingly at it.

"So what do you think happened to Evan?"

"You're his friend, you tell me. Speaking of which, I don't remember ever meeting you. If I had I think I would have remembered."

Her gaze shifted from her fingernails to me.

"I'm new in town, but your husband and I were friends in college."

"And Valerie hired you, I get it." The way she said it suggested there was no love lost between the two. "She send you here?"

I nodded. She propped herself up on her elbows.

"He cheated on me, you know. Did you know that?"

I shook my head.

"I don't care, I cheated on him too. It doesn't matter. It's a no fault divorce, like a car accident. I don't hate him, you know."

"I'm sure you don't."

"People said I married him for his money. Maybe I did. I guess that was part of it, but we had a couple of good years."

"When was the last time you lived together?"

"Really lived together? About a year ago, then he moved into that pool house." She rolled her eyes and shook her head. "I guess he's happy there, who wouldn't be? It's like the best property in Miami."

She reached down and scratched her foot. It made me lose my train of thought.

"Can you tell me a little about his involvement with the family firm?"

"What is this, twenty questions?"

"If he's mixed up in something, anything you could tell me might be a big help. Strictly confidential, of course."

"If you must know, Evan didn't know anything about the steel business, or real estate for that matter, but it looked good to parade a family member out to customers at trade shows and stuff like that. Evan only had a small stake in the company, you know, there were other investors. Real pains in the ass, Evan said, not like the old days. Then when he started complaining about the management, they threw him out."

"Complaining how?"

"Said it was being mismanaged. Too much real estate speculation. Turns out he was right, I guess. He may not have been much of a business executive, but he wasn't an idiot. Anyway, you didn't hear it from me, not that I care. The management didn't need him criticizing them behind their backs, so they just got rid of him. Just as well, Evan really wasn't interested in the business."

"What was he interested in?"

"Other stuff. Business ventures. Drove me crazy. Lost a lot of money over the years, too. You probably know all about it, being friends and all." She lowered her dark glasses and looked at me. "Guess the eccentricity runs in the family."

"How so?"

"Well his great gramps made all the money, then the rest of them were free to indulge. Evan's dad spent most of his time in Nepal, did you know that? Studying their art. He was a hippie. His grandfather liked horses. And Evan went for the whole Jacques Cousteau thing. And don't ask me for details, I lost interest years ago. I mean, it was sexy when we were dating, then it became such a joke."

"Who might know more about it?"

"Try his girlfriend. Evan was seeing a woman named Regina. He probably used all the Jacques Cousteau stuff on her. She owns a spa in Coral Gables."

"I already spoke to her."

"Oh yeah, well if you see her again, tell her I said 'hello.'"

"Thanks, I will."

"I hope you find Evan. I hope he's okay." She paused, giving me one last look. "Why don't you give me your card? Isn't that what detectives do, in case I think of anything?"

ELEVEN

Earl's Boatyard was a hold-out from old Miami - a ramshackle place on Snapper Creek Canal in South Miami that the proprietor, Earl Montgomery, had probably inherited from his father, who probably got it from his father when Miami wasn't much more than a backwater trading post on a mosquito infested coast. It took more than a single generation to achieve that level of rust and dilapidation.

Miami had evolved, Earl's hadn't.

It was raining when I arrived. I zipped up my tracksuit and rushed in from the car. The boatyard fronted a sleepy inlet and consisted of a tin-roofed building and a dock where they dispensed diesel fuel and gasoline. Inside was a lounge, I guess you could call it, with ratty furniture, a tank where live shrimp were sold as bait, and a counter presided over by a big woman with flabby arms. Behind the counter were basic supplies like shaving cream and fishing lures, as well as some mail slots. I guess the woman served as an unofficial postmistress for visiting yachtsmen.

I looked around at the room's nautical kitsch: the mounted swordfish, the lobster buoys and old nets, the sign pinned to the wall that read "Wanted: Good woman who likes to go fishing, clean fish, dig worms, cook. Must have boat and motor. Please send picture (of boat and motor)."

"Earl around?" I asked the woman with flabby arms.

She pointed to a chess game in progress.

Earl was probably in his early fifties, but looked older because of the weathered skin and gray beard. He was sitting on a red plastic milk crate playing chess with a man in a polo shirt with the name "Temptress" stitched on the breast pocket. These embroidered shirts seemed to be all the rage. Earl's opponent studied the board while Earl absently watched raindrops splashing down on the dock. He kept his index finger on the bishop's head while deciding where to move it.

Outside, there was a 40-foot sloop tied up at the dock, clean and polished, built for speed. She had a shiny white hull with the name "Temptress " in gold letters on the transom.

"Looking for me?"

Earl had the gravelly voice and deep southern accent of a native Floridian. He studied the board, more interested in the game than me.

"I'm looking for Evan Salisbury, actually, I was hoping you might be able to help me."

"Evan Salisbury?"

I nodded.

"This about that shooting? What's the boat called?

"Rum Runner."

"You a detective?"

"My name's McCoy. Salisbury was a friend of mine, I'm looking for him."

"Can't be too good a friend if you have to ask where he is."

"He's gone missing, the family's concerned."

"Missing, huh?"

"That's right," I said. "So do you mind if I ask you, when was the last time Rum Runner was here?"

"I guess I seen it maybe a week or so ago. It took on fuel."

Temptress, after much deliberation, moved his bishop,

73

threatening Earl's rook. He watched Earl carefully, waiting for the countermove. In a decisive gesture, Earl exchanged bishops.

"Other than that, you ever talk to him?"

"Can't say that I did."

"But you know him?"

"Not really, like I said, just seen him 'round a few times. Crew took care of the boat. Always had a crewmember take care of everything."

Temptress concentrated on the board. There were beads of perspiration on his upper lip. Again, he rested his index finger tentatively on his knight's head, then ever so slowly, his eyes on Earl, he cautiously removed the finger. Earl moved his queen diagonally across the aboard, plopping it down audibly.

"Check," said Earl, raising an eyebrow to see what his opponent thought of that.

Temptress blocked Earl's attack with his own queen only to be forced into an uneven exchange. Then one of Earl's pawns chased the king across the board, and the inevitable checkmate was delivered by the knight. Temptress studied the board for some time to make sure there was no way out as thunder rumbled in the distance. He shook his head and tossed a five on the board. I cleared my throat.

"I was told that he found his crewmember here, Andrew Bigelow. Young guy, about six feet tall, blond hair?"

"Lots of people use the bulletin board for stuff like that."

"So you didn't know Andrew?"

"Name don't mean nothin' to me." Earl crossed his arms. He had tattoos on his forearms. One of them was a dragon, another a fouled anchor.

"Someone told me there was another person, Clifford Mink, who worked on his boat, a mechanic, I believe. She said Salisbury knew him from here. Is he around?"

"Cliff Mink? Nah, he ain't been around for a while."

"Any idea where I can get a hold of him?"

Earl shook his head.

"I might be able to help," said Temptress. "I remember Rum Runner, who wouldn't? We were tied up alongside her for a while when our boat was having its engine tuned. This is about two or three weeks ago. I remember because I talked to the guy who was washing and waxing the boat about doing some work for me. I have his card, in fact."

He dug into his wallet and produced the card. It was the kind that you print yourself on an inkjet. It read "Clifford Mink, marine maintenance. Class D truck lic." and, as luck would have it, there was an address.

"He was working on Rum Runner?" I asked.

"Yeah."

"Did he come to work for you?"

"Not yet, but I'm thinking of it, looked like he did a good job. I never met your friend though, just some kid worked on the boat."

I took out my notebook and copied down Mink's address and phone number.

"That would have been Andrew," I said.

"Nice kid."

"Yeah, he was."

Amazing how observant you get when someone's trying to kill you, you notice a car driving too slow, a man sitting on a bench waiting for a bus, or someone reaching into a bag of donuts, anything that might indicate

75

homicidal intent. Even a bumper sticker on a car that says "my kid is an honors student," because that means the car's probably safe, unless, of course, that's what they want you to think.

Paranoid or not, I was pretty sure someone in a silver Cadillac Escalade was following me, and not doing a good job of it. At a stoplight I even managed to take note of the plate, and then was able to shake them in downtown traffic. At least I thought I had shaken them.

I was ticking down my list of leads, meeting with people who knew or were close to Evan Salisbury. By the end of the day, I hoped to have assembled a good picture of what he had been doing prior to the shooting. I was also new at this, and wanted to make sure I put in $500 worth of labor.

Michael Arnett, CEO of Salisbury Holdings, occupied a corner office overlooking Bayside Park, just north of the Intercontinental Hotel. Maybe the headquarters of Salisbury Holdings had once been grand, even stylish - mod chrome furniture and lighting fixtures - but now the carpet was frayed and coffee-stained, the curtains and upholstery faded and dated. It was cluttered with mismatched filing cabinets and storage boxes. There were just a few workers, and the place had the look of a quiet back-office accounting operation. Arnett's assistant, a young man in a blue blazer and a bad haircut, showed me to his office. Arnett sat at his desk in his shirtsleeves. His tie was loosened and his sleeves rolled-up.

"What do you need to know?" he said as I planted myself in a black leather chair across from him. He sounded like he had more than a few things on his to-do list, and talking to me wasn't one of them.

"I gather the company's been around a long time. The

grandfather started it?"

"I didn't know we were going to start at the beginning. Okay, yeah, August Salenbach. You're going way back."

"Salenbach?"

He swiveled his chair around and pointed at an imposing portrait on the wall.

"They Americanized the name a long time ago. The company changed from Salenbach Steel to Salisbury Steel. Sounded more American, went better with his mansion in Coconut Grove."

"And now it's mostly real estate investments?"

"When the market for American steel tanked, the family started diversifying. Real estate is one component, other things too. We're not even in steel fabrication anymore."

"And dare I ask how the company's doing?"

"Like most everybody else, not great. Let's just say we've been experiencing negative cash flow results the past few quarters. We filed for chapter 11 two months ago. We'll be reorganized, and we'll hang on, but we'll emerge as a different organization."

"How so?"

"Smaller, leaner, managing the properties we keep, letting some revert to the banks." He steepled his fingers and sounded very sure of himself. "The company has been around for many years, adjusting as the times dictated, and we'll be around for many years to come."

"So, bankruptcy?"

"As I said, I prefer to describe it as a reorganization." He smiled.

"Would it help if Evan came back?"

Arnett leaned back in his chair. "Probably not, to be honest. He serves on the board, but he has no operational control, not anymore."

"So he used to run things?"

"Couple years ago, before I was brought in. A company like this needs expert management."

"And that's you?"

"That's me."

"How involved was Evan in the new business model?"

"He bought into it, for the most part. In fact he spearheaded a number of successful projects around town. Mostly small apartment buildings, condos. He was pretty good at those, renovated a few art deco hotels on the beach back in the '90s, from what I understand."

"When was the last time you saw him, for the record?"

"A few weeks or so ago, at a shareholders' meeting."

"Notice anything unusual?" I asked.

Arnett shook his head. "No."

"His girlfriend mentioned a property he built out in the Everglades. What was that all about?"

Arnett looked confused. "The Everglades? No, we don't own anything west of I-95."

"Hmm. I wonder what that's about. Would it be possible to have a list of the company's holdings, particularly the ones Evan was involved with?"

"Sure, no problem."

He got up from his desk and walked over to a file cabinet and found a print-out of the company's real estate portfolio. He marked it up to indicate which properties Evan handled, then handed it to me, told me I could keep it.

I thanked him and got up to leave. "In the event he was kidnapped, it's possible they'll get in touch with you. I don't think that's the case, but call me if anything happens."

"You'll be the first to know."

He handed me his card. I handed him mine, the one that read Harry McCoy, attorney at law, with my old New York address. I had crossed out the old address and penciled in my cell phone number and the name of the marina. Very professional.

"One last thing, does Evan still get along with the other members of the board?" I asked.

Arnett shrugged and turned his palms up. "What can I tell you, family businesses. Twenty years ago Salisbury Steel grossed over 100 million, last year we lost six. Would you be happy?"

TWELVE

Later that afternoon when I returned home it was still about a hundred degrees out. I checked the icebox. It was slim pickins. A jar of mayonnaise, some Pabst Blue Ribbon, and olives. In the cupboard I found crackers and a tin of sardines. I mixed the sardines with the mayo and made little sandwiches with the crackers. I washed them down with the beer. While I was eating, Virginia returned. This time she had Cameron with her. She was wearing the same baseball cap and a sundress with bare arms.

"I was just having a little snack, care to join me?"

"Maybe some other time," said Virginia. "What have you been up to all day?"

"If you must know, a client, Valerie Shoupe, hired me to locate her brother."

Virginia turned to Cameron and prodded her in the thigh.

"So you are a detective?" said Cameron.

"Not exactly. I'm a lawyer, or I was, now I have exactly one client." I put my plate of crackers down. "What's all this about?"

Cameron started to speak, then hesitated. Virginia spoke for her. "We had an incident while you were gone."

"It's my ex-boyfriend," said Cameron.

"What about him?" I asked.

"He came here this morning, while I was out." Her face grew taut, and she took a deep breath.

"He took Siegfried," said Virginia.

I must have looked confused.

"My dog?" said Cameron.

"Why would he do that, is it his?"

"It was ours. It's mine now. He's trying to get back at me."

"I think you should call the police."

She started to tear up. I didn't like where this was going.

"It won't do any good," she said. "In fact it will make life even more difficult. He'll get angry. I don't want trouble, I just want my dog back. Anyway, the cops are all his friends. He owns a restaurant, a bar, where they all go."

"I see," I said, but I didn't really.

"But you could help her," said Virginia.

"Hang on a minute. I used to work in the DA's office, but we didn't handle this kind of case. And the key words there are 'used to.' Hell, I'm not even licensed to practice law in the state of Florida."

"But you're obviously good or that other woman wouldn't have hired you. And you shot that man. You sound like the perfect person to help. I can pay you, too," said Cameron.

"Like I said, I'm not really taking clients. You're asking me to steal something. I'm a lawyer."

Virginia glared at me. "Lawyers steal all the time."

Cameron looked disappointed.

I didn't know what else to say, so I took a deep breath. "Okay, where's this restaurant?"

Cameron's ex owned a busy rib joint in the Grove, with a packed bar and a line waiting for tables. It looked like a gold mine, judging from the number of flat-screen TVs mounted around the bar and dining room. There was a soccer match on one, and golf on another. The rest were

Major League baseball. The walls in the bar were decorated with photos of fishermen. The pictures that caught my eye were of giant tuna leaping out of the water to eat smaller tuna used as bait. There were also football photos, team photos, and individual portraits of football players. That's when I realized who Cameron's boyfriend was: Donny Peterson, sometimes referred to as the Pretzel Maker, former all-American, all-pro offensive tackle with a reputation for sending opponents off the field on a stretcher.

The list of teams he'd played for was almost as long as his list of DUI arrests and bar brawls. I recalled that he worked, briefly, as a professional wrestler, competing under the same name Pretzel Maker Peterson, after being released by the Oakland Raiders. The wrestling hadn't lasted long, he'd injured his back doing a backwards take-down off the ropes.

I found an empty stool at the bar and ordered a Beck's from a burly bartender who looked like he might have been recruited from the same offensive unit. I was just finishing my Becks when I noticed Peterson enter the bar. He was carrying Siegfried tight with both hands, like a football. He spoke to the bartender, the bartender tried to pet Siegfried. Siegfried snapped at him. The two men laughed. I left a few bucks on the bar and went to my car and waited for Peterson. I was hoping I could avoid direct confrontation with the Pretzel Maker. Forty-five minutes later Peterson left the bar. He walked to a vintage Mercedes, threw the dog in the back seat and got in. He drove away. I followed. A few blocks later he pulled into the parking lot of a place called Rubin's Gym. He parked the car and got out.

I sat in the car, with the top down, and thought about it

for a few minutes. Then I got out of the Rabbit and walked past his Mercedes, noticing he hadn't even bothered to crack a window. Siegfried was in the back seat, looking out the rear window, his paws on the arm rest. His small tongue was dangling out of his mouth and he was panting. I returned to my car, flipped open my cell phone and called directory assistance, who connected me with the gym.

"You've got a customer in there who just left his dog in the car with the windows up. If he doesn't let in some air I'm calling the cops."

"Who is this?"

"It doesn't matter who I am. What matters is your customer getting out here and opening the window."

I hung up.

Ninety seconds later Peterson walked out of the building. He had changed into a sleeveless shirt, leather weightlifter's belt and boots and looked like a circus strong man. He looked around the parking lot. I had adjusted myself so I couldn't be seen, ducking below the dashboard and watching through the side view mirror. I watched Peterson walk to his car. He unlocked the door and opened the rear window about two inches. Then he scanned the parking lot again with a mean look on his face and went back into the gym.

I waited a few minutes in case he came back out, then I took a wire hanger from the laundry in the backseat and got out of the car. The window of the Mercedes wasn't open wide enough for me to reach my arm in, so I used the hanger to try to hook the lock. I had to adjust it several times, but on the fourth try the door unlocked and I opened it. Siegfried sat there watching.

"Come on boy, let's go home."

Siegfried jumped as far away from me as he could get, ending up behind the back seat under the rear window. I climbed all the way into the car and grabbed him. Of course, Peterson was there when I climbed out of the car. He looked both confused and angry.

"I lowered the goddamned window, what the fuck?"

"This dog belongs to Cameron Blake. I have the documentation to prove it."

"What are you, some kind of doggie detective?"

"I represent Miss Blake, if you interfere, we'll charge you with violating your restraining order. I'd advise you to let it go."

"I advise you to shut your mouth and stay the fuck out of my car."

It was precisely the situation I had hoped to avoid. I figured I wouldn't be able to talk my way out of it. That left either fight or flight, or, more likely, a panicked combination of the two.

Before I could move he threw a left hook at me. I dropped Siegfried and ducked, but the blow hit me on the side of my head. I shook it off, stepped forward and hammered a left jab at his face, then a two-three at his mid section. It was like hitting a stack of sandbags. I realized I was in serious trouble. Dog or no dog, it was time to initiate the flight portion of my strategy.

I ducked a right uppercut which would have ruined my day if not the entire week, and countered with a right hook to his jaw. He stepped back as if nothing had happened.

"The dog's running away," I yelled, hoping to buy a few seconds, then I turned and ran. Peterson followed a few paces behind, but for the moment he seemed more interested in the dog than in me. I ducked behind a Ford F-150 van. Peterson didn't notice and ran ahead. I doubled back, jumped in the Rabbit, and started the engine. I drove as fast as I could out of the parking lot. My shirt was wet with perspiration, and my heart was beating in the red zone. I was half a block away when I checked the rear view mirror. I heard panting and looked down. There, on the back seat, was Siegfried.

The reunion at the marina was joyful. Cameron embraced and kissed the dog, then embraced and kissed me, though not as warmly.

"Did you have any trouble?"

"A little bit."

"Donny?"

"You didn't tell me he was the Donny Peterson."

"Maybe I should have mentioned that."

"Would have been helpful."

"I'm sorry."

"I'd be careful," I said, "something tells me we haven't seen the last of Donny Peterson."

THIRTEEN

The next morning, I was sitting aboard Hobo, drinking my first cup of coffee and watching a passing motorboat that might or might not have looked suspicious, when I got a phone call from Lopez. He said he'd tracked down an address in Kendall for Salisbury's partner, Bernie Leach. He gave me the info and we agreed to meet later that morning. He said he had a few things to do first. I decided to arrange a meeting with a lawyer friend of mine, Vance Redfield.

Vance and I went way back. We'd met in law school. He'd built a lucrative practice in downtown Miami after being rejected by all the big local firms. If you met Vance Redfield you understood why the fancy firms didn't want him within 500 yards. Vance Redfield was a slob. He must have weighed 275 pounds, his hair was always uncombed and his suit usually stained. Not exactly what you'd call a "rainmaker."

His clients were mostly crooks, which meant there was always a steady stream of business. Over the years, he'd made a name for himself, and developed an impressive network of contacts in the police department, DA's office, and Miami underworld. If there was something shady going on in South Florida, chances were Vance Redfield knew something about it. Chances were he represented one of the bad guys.

He agreed to meet me at a place called Sonny's, on South Beach, a restaurant that served breakfast and catered to undernourished models and European jet setters.

I chose a table on the terrace with my back to the corner

and a good view of the sidewalk. It was below a ceiling fan, which was also good. I flagged down a waiter, ordered an iced coffee and watched what few pedestrians there were on Ocean Drive. You don't find a lot of morning people on South Beach. Vance arrived. He spotted me and started squeezing past the tables, jostling a woman who was drinking a cup of coffee. He ignored her and kept moving.

Vance wore a white business shirt without a tie. The shirt was plastered transparently to his chest. Rivulets of sweat cascaded down the side of his head. He didn't belong anywhere near the tropics. He plopped down in a chair and ordered a full breakfast. "Evan Salisbury, huh?"

I nodded.

"And let me get this straight, you represent Valerie Shoupe?"

"Right again."

"She's one hot ticket."

"You know her?" I asked him, surprised.

"I've seen her."

"Socially?"

"Yeah, right. So what have you got yourself into?" he asked.

"I was hoping you might be able to shed some light on that."

Then I started at the beginning, and didn't leave anything out. Vance was shoveling fried eggs into his mouth, there was yolk on his chin. He wiped it up with the back of his hand.

"The guy you shot was named Demetri Popov?"

"I'm told he worked for Juri Epstein."

Vance choked on his coffee.

"Bad?" I asked.

"Not good."

"What do you know about him?"

"Let's just say you might want to leave town. Like immediately. No shame in that."

"I'd need a pretty good reason."

Vance stirred more sugar in his coffee. "He made his money on the black market in Moscow. Word is he's still the moneyman in all sorts of illegal activity, mostly overseas. I don't think he'd be too keen on you poking around his business dealings. He pretends to operate legit businesses, 'course that's all cover. Needless to say his businesses do very well.

I guess he moved here after he got squeezed out of Russia. The competition over there can be brutal, even for Epstein. Anyway, he's been working on his image for the last few years, says he made a fortune in Black Sea real estate. He gives to local charities, and politicians. I guess people figure everyone played hardball in Russia when communism fell, so they cut him some slack. Besides, the Russians scare people."

"Why would he order one of his people to kill Evan Salisbury?"

He held his palms up in the universal sign of ignorance. "It does seem risky from a PR point of view. Maybe this guy Demetri was doing some freelancing."

"I thought about that too."

"Still, you got a gangster like Juri, and what, couple of dead bodies and one missing multi-millionaire, you gotta assume, for safety's sake, he's connected to it somewhere. Who's handling the case?"

"Detectives Muldoon and Esperanza."

"Muldoon's okay, don't think I've met Esperanza."

"If you had you would remember. So if I wanted to

arrange a meeting with Epstein, how would I go about it?"

"Into the lion's den, huh? You don't mess around."

"What have I got to lose?" I asked.

"What are you gonna do, just show up and say 'excuse me, did you try to kill Evan Salisbury?'"

"Not in so many words."

"What words did you have in mind?"

"I was going to be very polite. Either he's not involved and will cooperate, or he is and I'll spook him and see what he does."

"Or you end up dying a painful death under very suspicious circumstances. Maybe you just up and disappear one day. But don't worry, I'll know what happened. Want my advice?"

"Sure."

"Pack up that boat of yours and get the hell out of Miami."

"I'll settle for a meeting with Epstein."

"Why are you doing this?"

"I asked myself the same question. I'll let you know when I figure it out."

Forty-five minutes later Lopez met me at the marina parking lot. He took one look at my car, with the windshield broken where the bullet went in, and my amateurish duct tape job.

"We'll take my car," he said.

The engine sounded like a pack of hungry wolves as Lopez threw the car into gear and we did a skidding turn out of the garage onto Brickell and roared down the street. He came to a stop at a red light. I took a deep breath and relaxed my grip on the armrest.

"You used to watch 'Starsky and Hutch' when you

89

were a kid, right?" I asked.

"No, why?"

"Never mind."

Lopez looked at me. "So Peterson hit you hard? Man, oh man, Pretzel Maker Peterson."

"Felt like I got hit by a 2 x 4. Thought I broke my jaw."

"Wouldn't be able to talk if your jaw was broken."

"That's true. Is there a black and blue on my cheek?"

"Doesn't look too bad."

I rubbed my jaw. "So what'd you find out about Salisbury's business partner, Bernie Leach?"

"A lot. Spoke to a guy I know at Miami PD, he did some checking. Scotland Yard has a file on him. He's wanted for questioning in Europe, mail fraud."

"Mail fraud?"

"That's what he said."

"Operating out of where?"

"Until six months ago, Cayman Islands."

"What else did they say?"

"Born in London, 1960, parents divorced. Dad a longshoreman, mom worked in a pub."

"Prison record?"

"In and out when he was younger, then he smartened up and stopped getting caught."

"What's he been up to lately?" I was feeling better and better about my decision to bring Lopez on board. First saving my life, obviously, then the Glock, now good intel. But I wasn't so sure about his driving. He was averaging 60 in a 40 MPH zone, and jamming on the brakes at the lights. I was feeling nauseated.

"For the past few years he's specialized in milking rich folks," explained Lopez.

"Like Evan Salisbury."

"Yep."

"How?"

"Phony investments. Worked pretty well, too, after they're taken a lot of these guys are too embarrassed to say anything, keep their mouths shut instead of showing everyone how stupid they are. Got their reputations to consider."

"So there's no way of knowing how many he scammed?"

"I guess there was enough complaints he decided to move from London to the Cayman Islands."

"And from there to here."

"You got it, starts on a new scam."

"Which was?"

"Put together a plan to salvage gold from some French ship that he said sank off Spain when that dude Napoleon was pullin' all his shit."

"And the ship didn't exist?"

"It existed, but not the gold. Anyway, he raises the dough, way more than he needs, and then the expedition is a bust."

"For everyone but him."

"Oldest scam there is."

"And Salisbury was his latest victim."

"Could be."

"Should be interesting, I'm looking forward to meeting this Bernie Leach."

Thirty minutes later we arrived at the address in Kendall, a complex of half a dozen stucco buildings, each with four or five townhouses. A sign outside read "Cypress Suites, furnished apartments." It was a relief when the car finally stopped. I got out and rang Leach's doorbell. No one answered. We waited a few minutes, then walked across the spongy Florida lawn to the back of the condos. A cement cinderblock wall, about seven feet high, enclosed small private patios behind each unit. There was also an avocado tree that looked like it might just support my weight. I worked my way up the branches, which sagged almost to the point of breaking, avocadoes dropping to the ground, and pulled myself over the wall, scraping my stomach, and dropped down on the other side. Then I opened the gate for Lopez.

"Next time it's your turn."

"That's cool," he said.

The patio was furnished with a redwood table, a few chairs and a grill. I tried the sliding glass door that led to the living room, it was unlocked, and we went in. The apartment was furnished like a hotel room, no personal items, hotel/motel art, hotel/motel furniture. I shivered. It was as cold as a morgue. The air conditioner had been set very low.

Lopez saw him first. "Looks like we're too late."

A man, I figured he was Leach, lay on the floor between the couch and coffee table. He'd been shot in the head, a pool of blood had seeped into the beige carpet, turning it brownish red.

I knelt beside the body and pulled out his wallet. He was slightly overweight, with longish gray hair and expensive Italian leather loafers. He wore a gold ring on his pinky, and a Rolex watch, and smelled of a sour mix of blood, cologne, and decay. The driver's license confirmed his identity.

When the police arrived they secured the crime scene with yellow plastic tape. They took our statements and asked us to wait in the heat on the front lawn, where a few neighbors hovered beyond the tape. Muldoon arrived half an hour later.

"Detective Esperanza isn't coming?" I asked.

"Sorry, she had other plans. So who is this guy?" asked Muldoon.

I explained, and Muldoon listened carefully.

"Okay, I'm impressed. Too bad someone got to him before you did." Muldoon looked serious, and a little annoyed. "Next time, let us know, we could have gotten a unit out here right away."

"My guess is he's been dead awhile."

"Based on what?"

"The blood on the carpet is dry," I said.

"What else did you notice?"

"Well, since you ask, and this is just a hunch, but if I murdered someone here, I might toss the pistol in that drainage ditch."

Cons who knew what they were doing always discarded the weapon as soon as possible, at least that had been my experience. Since there was no gun in the condo, or in the grass outside the condo, I figured the drainage ditch was a good bet. Muldoon dispatched a couple of uniformed officers to check it out. They took their shoes and socks off and rolled up their trousers and waded into the ditch. We waited while Muldoon worked the scene, then I saw him talking to someone on his cell phone, then he walked over to us. He didn't look too happy.

"Lt. Halloran wants both you guys back to HQ, says he and you need to talk."

"Who's Lt. Halloran?"

"My boss."

"Is that a pretty firm invitation?"

"It is."

Half an hour later we were ushered into a conference room at police headquarters. We took our seats and then Lt. Halloran entered. He was highly scrubbed, manicured, not a hair out of place, and wore a twill suit, perfectly pressed. He sat down at the head of the table.

"Hello, thank you for coming, I'm Lt. Halloran, I'm overseeing the investigation. I take it you're..." he looked down at his pad of paper, "Harry McCoy?"

"I am."

He looked at Lopez. "And this is?"

"My associate, Steve Lopez."

"I see." He sniffed and arranged a pen and notepad in front of him until they were lined up perfectly with the edge of the table. I had a feeling we were going to get off on the wrong foot.

He flipped through the police report, turning the pages with the tip of his index finger and thumb, like he didn't like it, and ignoring everyone else in the room.

"From the looks of things, I'd say you were in a little over your head," he said.

"Excuse me?"

He looked up at me. "I'm not sure you know what you're up against."

"I appreciate your concern," I said.

His lip curled in a cold smile.

"My concern is for my investigation. You're probably wondering why I asked you here."

"I figured it had to do with the murder of Bernie Leach, just taking a wild stab."

"I'll be very honest with you. I'm thinking there may be too many chefs in the soup." He stared at me for a reaction, jutting his chin out and opening his eyes wide. He would have done very well in a staring contest.

"Soup?"

"The point is, we can't have you traipsing through our crime scenes interfering with our investigation."

"I'm conducting an investigation, too."

"Is that what you call it? I call it breaking and entering into a murder scene."

"How else was I going to discover the body?"

"Not to mention contaminating evidence," he said.

"I didn't contaminate any evidence."

"You were present at the goddamned crime scene. You walked on the fucking carpet, in your shoes!"

"I need to do my job."

"And I need to do mine. What I don't need is a former New York City assistant district attorney tripping through my jurisdiction screwing everything up."

"You can do that all by yourself."

He slammed his hand down on the table. Lopez looked surprised.

I continued. "If we hadn't found him you wouldn't know about the crime scene. You would have had to wait until a neighbor smelled something funny. Only by then a week would have passed. Now, thanks to me, you've got a fresh homicide on your hands, so, you're welcome. Only you're blowing whatever advantage you may have had by jerking me around in a conference room in police headquarters. Maybe you should be out looking for Evan Salisbury."

Halloran's closely shaved face was turning red. He gritted his teeth and leaned toward me. He looked like he was going to pop a blood vessel.

"I don't know how you handled things in New York, but you certainly don't need to give me lessons on how to conduct an investigation."

"It was just a suggestion."

"I have a suggestion for you. Why don't you tell me what the hell your client's been up to?"

"Valerie Shoupe?"

"I'm talking about Evan Salisbury."

"He's not my client."

He slapped the table again. He reminded me of my French teacher, Monsieur Renard. He used to hit the table a lot too.

"You know what I mean," said Halloran.

"What about him?"

"You have reason to believe he's still alive?"

"I'm working on that assumption."

"Based on?"

"The fact that I'm being paid to find him."

He shook his head and breathed deeply, letting the blood pressure in his skull normalize. "It hasn't occurred to you that he's probably dead somewhere with a bullet in his head?"

"Is that why you've given up looking for him? It's so much easer that way, isn't it?"

"What kind of game are you playing here, McCoy?"

"Game?"

"Tidying up after a friend, maybe?"

"What friend might that be?" I asked.

"Maybe your old school chum, Evan Salisbury? Or his sister, Valerie Shoupe?"

"What are you suggesting?"

"Just that it seems a little odd to me how you're so far ahead of this investigation, and yet you don't seem to have the slightest idea what's going on."

Halloran flipped open another file on the table, he was glaring at me.

"I know all about you. That's right, I know all about your record up in New York."

Detective Esperanza entered, opening the door and closing it quietly behind her. She stepped quietly to an empty chair.

"You missed the best part," I said.

"Yes, you're just in time, I was just reviewing Mr. McCoy's stellar record in New York." He was treading on thin ice.

A uniformed officer entered the room and passed a note to Halloran, who looked up at the officer. "They sure?"

"Yes sir."

Halloran turned to me. "Keeps getting more and more interesting. We recovered a weapon outside Leach's apartment. It was registered to Valerie Shoupe. I'm pulling her in for questioning. Now we'll see who's a wise ass."

FOURTEEN

"Harry, what's all this about?" Valerie asked me over the phone.

"Bernie Leach was murdered today, maybe yesterday, maybe a few days ago. They found a gun. They think it's the murder weapon, and it's registered to you."

"Bernie Leach?"

"I know a good criminal defense attorney, Vance Redfield. I'd like to get him in on this right away, if you have no objection."

"Can't you do it?"

"I think it would be better if it were someone else."

"There's a police car at the front gate. Shall I buzz him in?" she asked.

"Yes, but don't talk to him. Just let him bring you here."

"I still don't understand why you can't be my lawyer."

"Just trust me," I insisted.

"I do. Okay."

I got off the phone and called Vance. His office was just two blocks from police headquarters, so he arrived five minutes later, practically salivating at the prospect of having Valerie Shoupe, heir to the Salisbury business empire, as a client. He'd managed to find an unstained and pressed suit to put on. He took some breath spray from his pocket and sprayed his mouth. We were standing in the lobby of police headquarters when Valerie entered.

She was wearing a tightly wrapped white dress and oversized dark shades, like a movie star. There was a uniformed officer by her side. She took off her sunglasses and searched the lobby for a friendly face, then she saw me. Vance was standing beside me. We stepped forward and I introduced him.

"Don't you worry, Mrs. Shoupe, we'll get this sorted out in no time," said Vance.

Before she could say anything, Lt. Halloran arrived, aware that a news photographer was taking pictures.

"Mrs. Shoupe, I'm Lt. Halloran, thank you for coming in. I'm afraid we'll have to ask to take your fingerprints."

"We agree," said Vance, nodding.

She appeared stunned. She was either innocent or a very good actress. A lady cop escorted her away to be fingerprinted; when she returned we reconvened in the conference room. Vance asked for a few minutes alone with his client. I stayed in the room.

"So what happened?" he asked, leaning back in his chair.

"I didn't kill anyone, if that's what you mean," replied Valerie. "Whoever did must have stolen my pistol, I gave it to Evan to hold."

Vance put his elbows on the table. "Why would you do that?"

"I don't like guns in the house."

Vance looked at me. "So why'd you have it in the first place?"

"A boyfriend gave me the gun. He was big into the NRA, I took a course. Then we broke up, so I gave the gun to Evan."

"Someone did go through the pool house where Salisbury was living," I said.

Vance looked at me. "You report the break-in to the police?"

99

"Of course," I replied. "Muldoon knows."

"That's good," said Vance. "That leaves us with maybe someone stole the gun, or maybe Evan killed Leach. We'll set that aside for the moment. What do you know about the victim?"

She hesitated. It was one of those subtle hiccups that reveal a lot.

"You knew him?" asked Vance. He was very perceptive.

She nodded.

Vance held his palms up. "Well?"

She nodded again, then bit her bottom lip.

"Why do I get the feeling I'm not going to like this?" asked Vance.

"Bernie and I... dated. Briefly, about three months ago. We're both interested in horse racing, and other things. But I hadn't seen him in about two months."

"Why didn't you tell me earlier about your relationship with Leach?" I asked.

"I thought he was back in England. I thought, I hoped, the two of us were ancient history."

"When was the last time you saw him?" asked Vance.

"Two nights ago. He called me, said he wanted to talk. I agreed." She hesitated.

Vance pressed. "And?"

"I went to his apartment. "

"And?"

"We talked, then I left."

"Talked about what?" asked Vance.

She took a deep breath. "He was worried about Evan. Terrified. He said he'd been out of town, came back and heard about what had happened. He wanted to know if I knew what was going on."

"Why go to his place, why not have him come to you, or meet somewhere else?" asked Vance.

"I didn't want him at my house. I was afraid he wanted to get back together."

"Did he?"

"No."

"What did he know about Evan?" I asked.

"He said he didn't know anything. Said he would call me if he found anything out."

"Did you know about Leach's record?"

"Yes, he told me, but that was in the past."

"What time did you leave?" asked Vance.

"About a half hour after I got there."

Vance leaned forward. "And he was still alive?"

She looked him straight in the eyes. "Very much so." She turned to me. "Whoever killed him obviously stole the gun from the guesthouse. They probably followed me. I mean, that's obvious, right?"

I nodded. "I advise you to have Vance here do all the talking."

"Won't that make me look guilty?"

"Not in a court of law. Any inconsistencies in your statements can work against you, trust me."

She deflated into her chair.

"Okay, have it your way."

Vance went into the hall and told Halloran we were ready. Lt. Halloran entered, followed by a policeman and Detectives Esperanza and Muldoon.

Halloran dropped a yellow legal pad on the table and spoke. "I don't know what's going on here. All I know is I have two homicide victims and a person of interest who seems to think she needs two attorneys to represent her."

I cleared my throat, "and your point is, other than the

fact that you don't approve of a client's right to counsel?"

"My point is, somebody better start telling me what's going on."

Vance interjected. "We're prepared to make a sworn statement."

"Fine, we'll start from there," said Halloran.

Vance repeated what he had just been told, explaining how she had come to own the gun, given it to Evan to hold, and how she had been invited to Leach's house the night before."

I added into the record that Evan's house had been searched, and probably burgled. I referenced the police report I had made following my visit. Halloran's lip curled when I referenced the police report.

A uniformed police sergeant entered the room. He whispered something to Halloran. Halloran excused himself and left the room. He returned a few minutes later.

"Looks like you're free to go. Fingerprints on the weapon weren't a match." He didn't seem happy about it.

Valerie let out a breath and looked relieved.

Halloran continued. "Interestingly enough, prints on the gun match the prints taken on the boat and the guest house. Looks like Evan Salisbury is our prime suspect."

"Wouldn't you expect to find his prints on the weapon?" I asked.

"Sure, especially if he murdered Bernard Leach."

Vance and Valerie and I left the conference room and walked into the lobby alone.

"What does this mean? I'm so confused." she asked.

"It means you're not a suspect after all. The question is, how did that pistol get to Bernie Leach's house with your brother's prints on it?"

"Does this mean Evan's alive?" she asked.

"It might, but I never figured your brother for a murderer, so it leaves us back where we were before. Listen, I have some business to wrap up here. Can I put you in a taxi?" I asked.

"Will you call me later?"

"If you want me to."

She said goodbye to Vance and I walked her outside where I found a taxi. Then I went back into the police station and found Detective Esperanza in a lounge near the lobby. She was trying to buy a sandwich from a vending machine. The dollar bill was wrinkled, and the machine kept rejecting it.

"You're actually going to eat one of those?" I asked.

She smiled. She had a nice smile, that and a very small overbite which I hadn't fully appreciated before.

We sat at a Formica table near the vending machine where she pulled the plastic wrap off the sandwich.

"Valerie Shoupe is a beautiful woman," said Detective Esperanza.

"Yes she is."

"She's divorced?"

"Widowed."   -

"And she hired you to find her brother, just like that?"

"Unlike your boss, she seems to think I'm good at what I do. Can I ask you a question?"

"Sure."

"Is Halloran like that with everybody or has he taken a personal dislike to me?"

"He doesn't like private investigators, and he hates lawyers."

"Did he flunk out of law school or something?" I asked.

"Never made it that far."

"So why's he so interested in the case?"

103

"It's unusual. I'm guessing he's under pressure from above to get this one buttoned up."

"Why?"

She shrugged. "Salisbury was a big shot, Harry, high profile, and so is Juri Epstein. All I know is he's asking for status reports twice a day and it's driving Muldoon and me nuts."

"Charging Salisbury with Leach's homicide would never make it past a grand jury. Is Halloran planning a run for office?"

"Welcome to my world."

She took a bite of her sandwich, then stopped chewing. I didn't think she liked it.

"Harry, do you think it's wise for you to have her as a client?"

"Why wouldn't it be?"

"There's a contract out on you, that's why, and your life is in danger."

She gave up on the sandwich, wrapping it in a napkin. "Seriously, Harry, I don't want you getting in over your head. Nothing personal, but Miami can be a very rough town."

"So everybody keeps telling me." I wanted to change the subject. "Instead of vending machines, why don't you let me take you out to dinner tonight?"

"Dinner?"

"You and me."

"Harry, you surprise me."

"Does that mean no?"

She smiled. "It means yes, I'd like that."

"And meanwhile can I ask a favor?"

"What's that?"

I handed her a piece of paper from my notebook. "Can

you run this plate?"

"What is it?"

"Cadillac Escalade that's been following me. I think."

"Deal. And I'll see you at my house at 8 o'clock."

She wrote her address on her sandwich wrapper and slid it across the table.

FIFTEEN

I had a few hours of work yet. Lopez drove me home, where I hopped into the Rabbit. I scanned the print-out of real estate holdings Arnett had given me. The empire wasn't as vast as I had thought, but it was still substantial. The family owned interests in several luxury high-rises, several small hotels, and a few other developments.

The list was divided according to numerous independent corporations, controlled by various members of the family. One, Seaside Holdings, Inc., consisted of a dozen or so properties and was personally controlled by Evan Salisbury. I decided to start with those first.

My first stop was an art deco hotel on South Beach that was being renovated. The building was gutted, so I didn't even bother getting out of the car. The next was an apartment house on Collins that was vacant and surrounded by scaffolding. It appeared construction had been stopped. I crossed it off the list. The rest of the properties were single-family houses. Most of them were located in Coconut Grove, and were either boarded up with no signs of life or they appeared to be occupied by someone.

I had worked my way down two-thirds of the list and had begun to question whether the exercise was a waste of effort when I pulled up in front of a small Spanish style hacienda on Ponciana Avenue. There was a For Sale sign out front, and Evan Salisbury's real estate company was listed as the contact. The driveway led to a porte cochere on the side of the house. Through the porte cochere, tucked nearly out of sight behind the house, was a gold Mini Cooper that matched the description Valerie had given me. Evan Salisbury's car.

I parked in the street and walked across the lawn. On either side of the front door were box-shaped hedges that ran the width of the house. Behind them was a large picture window overlooking the lawn. I pushed my way through a tight gap in the hedges and peered through the window. The room was furnished as a model home. There was fresh-looking carpeting and a matching set of beige leather furniture, and no personal clutter.

I followed the cement path around the side of the house to the kitchen door and looked through the window in the door. The kitchen was empty, with new tiles and stainless steel appliances. The counters were bare except for a drip coffee maker. There was about an inch of coffee in the pot.

In the back of the house, I found a cement block patio around a swimming pool, and sliding glass doors leading to two bedrooms. The bedrooms looked like they had been staged for sale as well. In one there was a suitcase, and on the floor a small pile of dirty laundry. I tried both sliding glass doors. They were locked, so I went back to the kitchen and picked up a brick from the edge of the path and smashed a pane of glass in the door, then reached in and unlocked it.

The house smelled of fresh paint, plaster, and the new carpeting. On the kitchen table was a copy of Monday's Miami Herald. The coffee was cold. I opened the fridge. It was empty except for a container of yogurt and a quart of milk. I smelled the milk. It was sour.

I passed a bathroom on the way to the bedroom. On the sink was a toothbrush. I felt the bristles, and they were dry. Then I went into the bedroom. Among the dirty

107

laundry I noticed a blue tennis shirt. On the breast the name "Rum Runner" was embroidered. Salisbury had been here, and if I had to guess, he had left in a hurry two days earlier without his car.

It was good news. Actually, it was great news. It meant Evan had been hiding out, not dead. But for whatever reason, he had abandoned the model house in a hurry. But why would he have abandoned his car, I wondered? Whatever the reason, it meant he had been alive at least a day after Andrew Bigelow's murder. It meant I was getting closer, if only just a little. It also meant I could stop working my way down the real estate list.

SIXTEEN

The sun was just setting when I arrived at Detective Esperanza's house two hours later. It occupied one half of a two-story cement building near the south bank of the Miami River. Both sides of the river were cluttered with derelict vessels and brightly painted Haitian fishing boats. Her building had once been a fruit market. Faded paint on the façade read "Miami Fruit Co."

It was a drab industrial building, the front door protected by a steel gate, but when the detective opened the door she revealed a well-lit space within. Her smile was sunny, too. She'd changed into a light blue linen shirt, white jeans and leather flip flops.

She looked me up and down. "You look like you could use a drink," she said. "We'll have them on the roof, I have a nice view of the other side of Miami."

Her apartment was an open layout, the kitchen was connected to the living room, a mix of modern furniture and flea market finds, painted in turquoise and oranges.

"Have you lived here long, detective?" I asked.

"About three years, and please, drop the detective stuff. It's Consuela."

She collected two glasses and a lime and we started up the stairs. They led to a second floor sleeping loft, where a double bed with white gauzy netting was placed catty-corner on one side, an Eames chair and desk on the other. A quick glance at a packed bookshelf suggested she had a preference for spy thrillers and hardboiled detective novels. Narrow steps led to the roof where there was a small deck

109

and garden. There was a view of other rooftops, mostly old warehouses, and the river. The air was wet and warm. I could hear the claxon of horns from Calle Ocho in the distance, and Cuban music.

The sun was gone, there was just a pink glow silhouetting the riverfront buildings. A light breeze wafted in from the ocean. Consuela poured the drinks, sticking her tongue out between her lips as she measured out the rum.

"I found Evan Salisbury's car," I announced.

"Did you? I'm impressed, Harry. Where was it?"

"At one of his real estate projects in Coral Gables. Looks like he was staying there, but left without his car." I told her the address.

"You think he'll be back?"

"I think he left in a hurry."

She handed me my drink. "We'll need to check it out."

Consuela leaned against the wrought iron railing, the skyline of Miami behind her. A gentle breeze ruffled her linen shirt. "I have some information for you. I ran those plates," she said.

"And?"

"You're not going to like it. They're registered to a business owned by Juri Epstein. Did you happen to get a look at who was in the car?"

I shook my head.

"I don't like it Harry. Why would he be following you?"

"Maybe they want me to lead them to Salisbury?"

"Maybe, but given what I know about Juri Epstein, I'm more concerned for your safety. It sounds like someone's out for revenge. I might even have to take you into protective custody."

"Sounds like my lucky day."

110

She smiled. "We're dealing with one… two homicides and one missing person. Not bad even by New York standards. I don't want you to be the next victim."

"So you pull Juri in and squeeze him."

"Wish it were that easy. Epstein's out of town, he's also very powerful. But it's Demetri's cousin Junior who worries me. He's a sociopath, Harry. Take the toughest mobster you ever prosecuted up in New York, Harry, the biggest, baddest one you can remember, and then give him a good dose of steroids and you'll have Junior. He's the one I want to find. I hate the idea of him being out there, somewhere. I don't think Muldoon was so off base when he suggested you lay low for a while, even consider leaving town, or at least that marina. You're vulnerable there."

"I have Lopez."

"Who won't always be around."

I sat down in a metal chair. "Then I guess the sooner I find out what's going on the better. What else have the police turned up?"

"We know that Salisbury's company was a shambles, Chapter 11. That could have led him into some shady financial dealings. Who knows, maybe he owed Epstein money, or someone else, and they hired either Juri or Demetri to kill him."

I shook my head. "The business was in Chapter 11, but Salisbury still had dough. He wouldn't have had to go to a loan shark."

"Then why wouldn't Salisbury come to us, Harry? They missed him on the boat, he must have known he was the intended victim, why did he run?"

"Maybe he has something to hide. Maybe he has a problem with authority. Maybe he's sitting on a tropical island somewhere sipping – what are these, anyway?"

"Mojitos."

"They're very good." I took another sip. "I think maybe Salisbury wanted to skip town, pick up a few things, some clothes, some money, a weapon, but someone got to him before he could do that."

Consuela sat down in a chair beside me. "You think he was mixed up in something illegal?"

"None of the people I spoke to seem to think so."

"Then what?" she asked.

I shrugged.

"Muldoon thinks maybe it was a set-up, maybe even staged by Salisbury."

"An inside job?" I asked.

"No one knew where Salisbury's boat was docked, Harry. How would they have found Rum Runner?"

"Motive?"

"To disappear?"

"Sounds far fetched. You believe that?"

"My opinion is irrelevant."

"So you don't agree?"

"There are a lot of people in this town who would like to see Salisbury take a fall," she said.

"He has enemies?"

"He's rich, Harry, it's schadenfreude."

"Which reminds me, I'd like to have a look aboard his boat, but it was towed away."

"It's tied up at the Coast Guard station. I can put you through to the guy out there, Alex Rhinehart. He'll let you get aboard. Harry, I'm giving you the file on Juri Epstein, plus anything else we have. I think it would be a good idea if we continue working together, sharing information. I don't want you stumbling into something and getting yourself killed. I want to know where you're going, who you're talking to."

"Is that normal standard police procedure?"

"Call it pooling limited resources. I want to stay very close to you."

I smiled. "My client would have no objection."

She took a deep breath and let it out. "Let's get off the subject for a while. Enough detective talk."

"What do you want to talk about?"

"How about you?" asked Consuela. The drink was loosening her up.

"What about me?"

"You grew up in New York City?" she asked.

I shook my head. "Little town in upstate New York. Taunton Springs. You never heard of it."

"Farm town?"

"Adirondacks. My dad was in the state police. "

Her mouth opened in a surprised smile. "Your dad was a cop. So that explains a few things."

"Don't know about that, there wasn't much of a crime blotter in Taunton Springs, the occasional DUI, and sometimes a moose would stop traffic on Main Street."

She laughed. "So you have family in Miami?"

"An aunt and an uncle, a cousin too. My mom is my Aunt Mimi's younger sister. Aunt Mimi married Uncle Morris and moved down here. My mom met my dad in college, SUNY New Paltz. She stayed in New York."

"And you moved from Taunton Springs to the big city."

"Right."

"And now you're here."

"For another month or so."

"I read your bio, Harry. Northwestern undergrad, FBI academy, NYU Law, Manhattan DA's Office, pretty strong

113

credentials. Why'd you quit?"

"I lost interest, couldn't do it anymore. Besides, last time I looked I was still gainfully employed."

"Why'd you lose interest?"

"I was on a special task force, the Investigative Division, and I had a partner, Lucy Davenport. She was a cop, like you."

"And you fell in love with her and she broke your heart."

"Not exactly. Can we talk about something else? Anything else"

"Harry, I'm sorry, I didn't mean-"

"That's okay. Why don't you tell me about Muldoon."

She laughed. "Why do you want to know about him?"

"Because he interests me. Been partners for a long time?"

"About a year, ever since I came over from narcotics."

"Narcotics, you don't mess around."

"What would you expect me to be, a meter maid?"

"No, it's just that narcotics is, well, it's a rough racket, especially here in Miami."

Her mouth formed something between a smile and a frown.

"You're worse than the Cuban men I know."

"What's that supposed to mean?"

"You know damned well what it means. And if you must know, I thought about law school. I decided to go to the police academy instead. I like my job."

"What about your social life?"

Consuela raised an eyebrow. "Now women cops can't have a social life?"

"I've heard it can be difficult."

"I guess it is. Homicide can be a tough schedule. I get

asked out, sometimes I have to cancel."

I was starting to enjoy our conversation. I was certainly enjoying the company. The rum made me feel warm inside, balanced with the evening air.

"We'd better go or I'll have another drink and be drunk," said Consuela.

"I'll drive," I said, momentarily forgetting what it was I was driving. Outside her house, Consuela stopped short when she saw my car.

"Jesus, Harry."

The tape I'd used to repair the windshield hadn't worked, and I'd ended up removing the large loose chunks of glass from the frame.

"I take it you've never had a windshield shot out."

"Can you drive like that?" she asked.

"As long as we don't go too fast."

Her look of skepticism turned to laughter as I opened the door for her. Twenty minutes later I pulled up in front of Joe's Stone Crabs and handed the keys to the valet, who wasn't overly impressed by my ride either.

When we were seated I ordered crab claws, a side dish of creamed spinach, potatoes Lyonnaise and a bottle of pinot grigio.

"So you grew up in Miami?" I asked.

She nodded. "I went to parochial school, then University of Miami."

"Your parents are Cuban?"

"They came over in '59, when Castro took over. My father had been a judge in Havana, he started over here in Miami. He joined a law firm and eventually became a judge again. They live in the Cuban district, near Calle Ocho."

"You think they'll ever go back?"

115

"Maybe one day, when freedom is restored, but our old house is an apartment building now, and we don't have many family members there. It was a long time ago, Harry. I love Miami, and would never leave."

The stone crab claws arrived, and Consuela showed me how to eat them.

"What about you," she asked. "Do you miss Taunton Falls?"

"Taunton Springs. Sometimes, but I don't have family there anymore, and it's pretty quiet."

"So where's home?"

"Here I guess, or wherever Hobo is."

"You can't live on a sailboat forever."

"I know, but it works for now."

She dipped a crab claw in the mustard sauce. "Sometimes I wish I could do something like that."

"The time was right, I seized the moment. But if you see me a year from now, unshaven, barefoot, panhandling in Key West Harbor, do me a favor, will you?"

"What's that?"

"Arrest me."

She smiled. "Okay, but Key West's not my jurisdiction."

SEVENTEEN

A new day. There was a light rain falling, but I felt full of hope, which was a weird feeling for me. Maybe it was because no one had tried to kill me, maybe because I had found evidence that Evan Salisbury might still be alive. Maybe it was my dinner with Consuela. I rose early and met Lopez at his house. He was waiting out front, dressed in a pale blue Adidas soccer jacket and matching pants, with three stripes, and sneakers. He had a cell phone clipped to his waist and wore wrap around sunglasses. I noticed he was carrying a Colt 1911 instead of his usual 9mm. It was in a leather shoulder holster under his jacket.

"Why the .45?" I asked when I got into his car.

He smiled, "'cause they don't make a .46." Pause for dramatic effect, followed by a big smile. "Just a gut. I figured I'd beef things up a little. Where to?"

"Crandon Estates."

"You been wearing the vest?" he asked.

"As much as possible," I replied.

"Good."

Crandon Estates was a trailer park where Clifford Mink, the handyman from Earl's boatyard, lived. The clouds had blown over by the time we got there, but the air still smelled wet. There was a directory of residents pinned to a bulletin board outside the office. The list was covered in plastic, and fogged by the humidity. Mink's name was on the list. It said his space was E-36. There was no one in the office to ask where that was, so we looked for it ourselves.

I hadn't been in many trailer parks before, but had a feeling that Crandon Estates wasn't one of the better ones. The homes were sun-baked, the paint faded, grass unwatered, and the latticework was plastic. A woman in a tank top who was sitting in a folding chair smoking a cigarette eyed me with curiosity as I studied the signs, trying to get my bearings.

"Who ya looking for?" she asked.

"E-36."

"Keep going down Ponce de Leon, cross Brickell and turn left on Collins." All the paths in the park were named after major streets in Miami.

We walked down the hard packed dirt path separating the homes and found number E-36. The trailer was sitting on cement cinderblocks, the tires low on air. I knocked. When no one answered, I cupped my hands around my eyes and peered through the window pane in the door.

It took a few moments for my eyes to adjust from the bright sun to the dark interior. I stepped through overgrown weeds to a side window where the sun's glare was less severe. The room had gold colored wall-to-wall carpet and dark plywood paneling. There was a half-eaten pizza on the coffee table, empty soda cans and dirty laundry piled on the couch. A lamp on the end table had been overturned, its shade, dented, lay on the floor.

"You better have a badge or a gun."

I turned to see a woman. She was short and stocky with close-cropped hair and tinted glasses, and had a tattoo on her muscular forearm.

"You heard me, you got about five seconds to clear on out of here."

"Is this Cliff Mink's trailer?" I asked.

"Who the hell are you?"

118

"The name's McCoy. Who are you?"

"I run this facility. This here trailer park is private property."

"We're looking for Clifford Mink," I repeated.

"Did you try knocking?" she asked.

"Yes."

"The place looks like a mess," said Lopez.

"I guess the housekeeper ain't been around." She had trouble modulating her voice, everything came out as a shout.

I knocked again on the flimsy door. There was no answer. I looked at the woman in the tank top.

She shrugged. "Is it unlocked?"

I tried the knob. It turned. I pulled open the door and entered. The woman with the tattoo followed.

The atmosphere was unventilated, a fly buzzed madly and there was a sour smell of body odor, and maybe a hint of bug spray, and it was very hot. She passed through the living room and slid open the accordion vinyl bedroom door. That's when I saw the blood, splattered on the wall, and more, much more, soaking the carpet. His body lay crumpled in the narrow passageway, and he was dead, of course.

"Oh my God," said the woman. "It's Cliff.

I stared at his face. It looked like he hadn't shaved in a few days, his head was a tangle of black greasy hair. His teeth were stained by years of tobacco, and his eyes were open in a blank stare. I caught a whiff of booze, something sweet smelling, and cheap.

"Should we check his pulse," she asked.

"I wouldn't bother."

"You a cop?"

I shook my head. "I'm a lawyer, he's a private

119

detective."

I used my cell phone to call the police. I suggested the dispatcher alert Detective Esperanza. Then we sat in the shade of a willow tree at a picnic table near the trailer. There wasn't much more we could do.

"He was a friend of yours?" I asked.

"We used to have a drink or two."

I looked at her tattoo, a heart with a dagger in it. Under the heart was the name "Sheila."

"I'm Harry."

"I'm Margo."

"You seem very protective of the residents here."

"I try. Some of these people work, someone's gotta keep an eye on things, protect their property."

"When was the last time you saw Mink?"

"Yesterday, on his way to catch the bus to work."

"How do you know he was going to work?"

"Where else do people go at seven in the morning?"

"He didn't have his own car?"

"If you call that shit box a car." She gestured toward a faded Ford Taurus on blocks in an empty trailer lot nearby. There were no wheels on it.

"What was he like?" I asked.

"Cliff was a good guy. Worked hard, odd jobs, boatyard work, truck driver, a little fishing. Didn't take no drugs and didn't drink too much, far as I know he never been in any trouble. Paid three hundred dollars rent plus a month's deposit. Other than that we ain't too fussy."

She was telling me more about him when the cavalry arrived. This time it was sirens and two patrol cars followed by an unmarked Ford Crown Vic. I wanted it to be Consuela and Muldoon. Just my luck, it was Lt. Halloran.

120

He made us wait while he did his investigating. Consuela and Muldoon showed up a little while later, but Halloran was running the show. Finally he sauntered over to me.

"Funny timing," he said.

"How's that?"

"You showing up here same time, more or less, that he gets wacked. You always seem to be one step ahead of the police, why is that?"

"Just good at what I do, I guess."

"Yeah? Why do I get the feeling you're not telling us everything you know, McCoy?"

"I guess you're just very sensitive."

"Well I'll tell you what. You keep on doing what you're doing, and we'll follow. And you'll either end up dead, or you'll lead us to Evan Salisbury. Either way suits me fine."

He turned and walked away. Lopez approached.

"What did he say?"

"He's chumming the waters, and we're the chum."

EIGHTEEN

As much as I would have loved to hang around chatting with Lt. Halloran, we had places to be, and people to meet. Our next stop was the Everglades property Salisbury's girlfriend, Regina, had told me about. The directions she'd given me took us to the western edge of town, somewhere off the Tamiami Trail, past a sorry stretch of strip malls and fast food restaurants. It was where Miami ends and the Everglades begin, where alligators and turtles compete for space with trailer parks and cheap motels.

"You think his wife, Christina, has something to do with this?" asked Lopez.

I shook my head.

"Might be money in it for her if she was a widow, instead of an ex-wife."

"She's not the type. Besides, she'll probably be a widow or an ex-wife three times before she's done. But she's no murderer."

"What about the girlfriend? He tells her he don't want to get married. She's wasting her time with him, she goes nuts. Crime of passion."

"And hires a hit man in the middle of the night? I don't think so."

"Just shooting ideas out."

He drove for a while and I watched the scenery. We were approaching the outskirts of town. Empty fields interspersed with neighborhoods of inexpensive ranch houses. Lopez broke the silence.

"Can I ask you a personal question?"

"Please do."

"Why'd you get into law enforcement? I mean, law school, your uncle got a big house on Coral Cove, why not go into law, make the big bucks."

"My dad was a cop."

"Oh, I get it, and he wanted you to follow in his footsteps?"

"No, my dad never wanted to be a cop, least he never told me. Going to the FBI Academy was my idea."

"He must have liked it, though."

"He was killed when I was eleven."

"Killed on the job?"

I nodded.

"That's rough. I'm sorry."

"They never caught who did it. His body was found on the road in front of his police cruiser. The lights were still on, the engine running. They figured it was a felon he pulled over for speeding. I don't really like to talk about it."

I remembered it as if it were yesterday: the knock on the door, relatives filling the house, the governor shaking my hand at the funeral, Uncle Mo and Aunt Mimi spending a month with us in New York sorting out our lives.

"That explains a lot," said Lopez.

"Like what?"

"Your personality."

"How do you mean?"

Lopez shifted in his seat. "I noticed it the other day, sort of negative way of looking at things."

"You figured that out?'

"Know what else?"

"What?"

"You got repressed hostility."

"Repressed hostility?"

123

"Yep."

"Thank you Dr. Lopez."

"See, I'm Latino. We express ourselves. We don't bury it. More healthy that way."

"Well, if it's all the same to you, I prefer not to vent."

"That's cool."

We drove for about five miles, then turned onto a side road paved in crushed sea shells that ran along a canal. The road led 50 yards to a dusty unpaved parking lot and a dilapidated strip mall where a wooden sign advertised a "Gator Pit." Another sign advertised airboat rides. More crudely lettered signs pushed live shrimp and bait.

We pulled up in front of a sad looking red brick building with cheesy looking stained glass windows. Its name was advertised on a faded canvas awning: "Gator Pit, Home of the Original Gator Burger."

"We feed 'em at 11 o'clock, case you're interested," said a man in work clothes sitting in a plastic chair outside the restaurant.

"I'll have to come back with the family," I said as I entered.

The smell of stale beer and smoke was almost overwhelming. There were a few tables with dirty tablecloths and silverware, but no food, and the kitchen, which was visible through an open door at the end of the bar, was empty. An unshaven man in a ratty waiter's jacket was replenishing the peanuts at the bar where we sat. I ordered a Budweiser, Lopez asked for a Pepsi.

A man in coveralls sitting at the bar watched us for a while, snickering to the man sitting next to him. Finally he said something. "You ain't from the state, are ya?"

"How's that?" I replied.

He smiled in a knowing way to his friend, like he was playing a joke on me.

"You ain't from the state?" he grinned. "Fancy college boys from the state come down, think just 'cause they graduated college they can tell us how to run things. Hell, I lived in the Everglades my whole life."

Whoever these people were from the state he was referring to, I decided to tell him I wasn't one of them.

"I was looking for Edgewater Road," I said.

The bartender held the mug up to the light to check for spots. "This here's Edgewater."

"I'm looking for number 14?"

The drunk sitting at the bar now took an interest. He slid off his stool and approached me in a zig-zag pattern. He studied the address I had written on a piece of notepaper.

"That's right down the road," he said.

"That's enough, Derek," the bartender gave the man a sharp stare.

"You wouldn't have seen Evan Salisbury around?" I asked.

Derek started to speak. He was interrupted by the bartender. "Never heard of nobody by that name."

Derek looked at me, then at the bartender.

"Leave them folks alone, Derek." The bartender turned to me. "Sorry, can't help you."

The men in the bar went back to staring at their beers, the bartender to polishing glasses.

"Well, thanks anyway, I won't bother you any more," I said.

Lopez and I finished our drinks, left the bar and drove back up the way we had come. When we were out of sight I did a u-turn and doubled back, this time passing the Gator

Pit. Behind it there was an airboat tied up to a wooden dock on a canal. About twenty yards past that we came to an unpaved driveway that led toward two low buildings with corrugated tin roofs. Lopez turned down the driveway and parked.

There were no signs of life in the buildings. One was rusty and weather beaten, the other new, a one-story steel building. Regina had said that Salisbury had supervised the construction of a new building, and I figured this was the place. There was a single steel door that was locked, and a series of bays along one side. The bay doors were locked, too.

"I'll check around the other side, meet you at the far end," said Lopez. "Somebody comes along just shout."

There was a row of windows at the top of the wall along one side of the building. They were too high up for me to see through so I dragged over a discarded pallet and leaned it against the side of the wall, then climbed to the top for a better look. Inside it was dark, but I could make out a row of empty shelves and tables. Near the tables were several 50-gallon drums, some smaller plastic chemical containers and a coil of plastic tubing. The sun was reflecting on the glass, so I cupped my hands over my eyes and was looking in when my ladder gave way and I fell to the ground, hitting hard.

"The hell are you doing?"

I looked up. A large man in a greasy baseball cap and woodland pattern camouflage T-shirt stood above me. He was wiping his hands with an oily rag. Derek was behind him.

"I was looking for a friend of mine –"

"You ain't got no business 'round here."

I stood and started dusting myself off. His first

126

punch caught me off guard: a right hook to the jaw that sent me back to the dusty ground.

"This here's private property."

I got up again and opened my mouth to speak, but the fist came again, this time I ducked. The third punch connected, and I stumbled backwards against the corrugated steel wall of the building. His arms were like hydraulic hammers.

"Go easy on him, Odell," Derek said.

The next punch would be the last, I thought, as I backed away. He followed. I feinted a duck to the left, then moved right, connecting with a left to his nose that caused more surprise than damage. I followed with a right to the jaw. Odell paused and wiped the blood from his mouth. He looked at the blood on the back of his dirty hand and smiled. This was not going to end well.

I considered turning and running, but realized he would be on me before I could get two paces. There was a pipe, about four feet in length, lying on the ground with some other construction debris.

He took another step toward me. I ducked, picked up the steel pipe as he stepped forward. The pipe caught him in the groin, and he doubled over and grunted, curling up into a fetal position. Derek and I looked down at Odell, surprised at the sudden turn of events.

"Odell?" said Derek.

"He got me low."

"You okay?"

"No, dang."

"Odell, you okay?"

"I will be if you jest let me rest a spell."

Derek turned to me. "Why'd you have to go and do that?"   He picked up a discarded 2 x 4 and advanced

127

toward me. Lopez reappeared. He had his .45 aimed at Derek.

"Let's all take a deep breath," he said.

"He got a gun, Odell," said Derek.

"Let 'em go, then," said Odell, still doubled over on the ground.

I nodded to Lopez and limped back to the car, leaving Derek to tend to Odell. Twenty minutes later Lopez and I were lunching at a rotisserie chicken place called Florida Chicken Kitchen. My jaw hurt even more from getting hit again, and Lopez said now it did look swollen. It was giving me a headache too. I wanted to go home and turn on the air conditioner, shut the hatch and forget I'd ever heard of Evan Salisbury. But we'd come this far, and I didn't want to return empty-handed.

NINETEEN

We ate our chicken in silence, licking the sticky spices off our fingers. The day had turned into a bust. I threw a wing bone onto my plate.

"We have to go back," I said.

"You sure that's a good idea?"

"No."

"But we should go anyway?"

I nodded. "We've come all this way."

"Okay, but we don't split up this time."

This time Lopez turned down a crushed coral side street and approached Salisbury's building from the other side, avoiding the bar. We parked on a side road lined with shabby ranch houses and mobile homes. A pit bull in a front yard raced toward us, barking ferociously. He lunged at me, but he was chained to tree and the chain jerked him off his feet. He kept barking, and lunged again. The chain pulled him off his feet again. I was glad there was a chain.

Otherwise the neighborhood was quiet. When we got to the dirt driveway that led to Salisbury's building, I couldn't see any cars or people so we walked down the driveway. The place was deserted.

We checked the side of the building where I had earlier tried to look inside. There was a door with a transom window above it. The window was open. I made a stirrup with my hand and Lopez heaved himself up. He squeezed through the window, and I heard him drop on the other side. The door opened. I went in.

The building consisted of one large room, lit by

windows in the roof. There were four large rectangular fiberglass tubs, and three rows of lab tables with bottles of chemicals on them.

Lopez looked at the lab equipment.

"Meth lab?"

I shook my head.

There were objects, rocks, piled on one of the tables. I picked one up. It looked like something encrusted in coral. I smelled it. It had come recently from the sea. I put it in the big pocket of my cargo shorts and knelt down to examine some plastic containers on a shelf under the table and read the labels.

"What is all this shit?" asked Lopez.

"Sodium hydroxide."

"You sure this isn't a meth lab?"

"I don't know."

I was still trying to make sense of the labels on the plastic containers when I heard a door close followed by the sound of a shell being chambered in a pump shotgun. It's one of those sounds that really gets your attention.

"Boys, I know I told you this here is private property." It sounded like Odell.

I raised my hands up. Lopez did the same.

"You just can't keep away, can ye?" It was Odell, the man with arms like pistons on a locomotive.

"It's not what you think," I tried to explain.

"Shut up, or I'll finish you both off here and feed you to the gators. Don't think I wouldn't."

"Look, when we met earlier, I think we got off on the wrong foot."

"I said 'shut it.'"

He nodded toward the door, indicating that we should

go. He followed close behind, prodding me with the shotgun.

"Easy with that."

"I said shut your mouth, fore I shut it for you."

He prodded us further down the driveway away from the main road to a neighboring house. There was a large yard behind the house. The yard fronted a canal, in the yard was a muddy pool, and in the muddy pool I could see the scaled back of an alligator, or was it a crocodile? No, I was pretty sure it was an alligator.

The back door of the house opened and a woman in a housedress came out.

"Whatcha got there, Odell?" she asked.

"Same prowlers was here before. Broke in, got 'em red handed."

"Whatcha gonna do?"

"I was fixin' to give 'em to Tiberius."

Tiberius, of course, was the alligator.

I looked at Lopez. "Cue the banjo music."

Lopez was calmly watching the shotgun, but he didn't have a move. Not yet, anyway. The gun was pointed at me, and the man's strength was evident. It would be difficult, if not impossible, to wrestle the gun away from him without something bad happening.

"Why don't you call the police and ask them about us, or better yet, call Mr. Salisbury if you know where he is. And if you do I'd appreciate letting me know. His sister's very concerned about him."

"The police got no business here."

"So what are you figuring on doing, Odell?" I asked.

"That's for me to know and you to find out."

He opened a gate in the chain link fence that surrounded the gator pit and gestured for us to enter.

131

"Won't be no problem if you holt real still. He's attracted by movement. I want y'all to empty your pockets, real slow."

Lopez and I did as we were told, disgorging our wallets and what cash was in our pockets on the other side of the fence. I threw down my 9mm, and Lopez his .45. The alligator remained motionless. It was about 50 feet away. I figured I could hop the fence if I had to before he was onto us, and so I kept an eye on the gator. That was what Odell must have had in mind. We were being guarded by the alligator, giving him time to lower the gun and check our IDs.

"Private investigator?" he asked.

"That's right," replied Lopez.

"For real?"

"Licensed by the State of Florida."

"This here says you're from New York. District Attorney's office. You a lawyer?" He said it like he'd just eaten a piece of sour fruit.

"I represent the Salisbury family. I've been hired to find him."

"How do I know you're telling the truth?"

"If you're concerned call the police, Detective Esperanza, in Miami." The alligator's tail sloshed in the water. "You know Mr. Salisbury?"

"Yeah, I know him. If you's his friend why'd you break into the place?"

"I told you, I've been hired by his sister to find him." I was taking a chance, for all I knew Odell had Salisbury hidden in a pit in his basement, slowly starving to death, and he would now kill me, but something told me otherwise.

He turned to Lopez. "For real?"

132

Lopez nodded.

"Wha'd you say your name was?"

"I didn't, but it's Harry. Harry McCoy."

"Thing is, we had couple guys poking 'round here the other day, can't be too careful. Mr. Salisbury don't like no prowlers. I reckon you guys are ok." He turned to the house. "Sugar, I reckon they're ok, I'm fixin' to let 'em go."

The woman in the housedress reappeared on the porch. "You don't let them go without asking them if they want tea! You got better manners, Odell."

"Y'all want tea?"

"I think what we'd really like is to move away from Tiberius."

"Hell, he ain't gonna hurt no one. I just done fed him a chicken."

We drank the tea on the back porch. It was actually iced tea and very cold and tasty.

Seeing as how our relationship was now on a more social footing, I asked him when he had last seen Salisbury.

"Reckon 'bout a week ago. Unloaded some boxes and sech."

"You spoke to him?"

"I speak to him ever' time he come up here. I keep an eye on the place."

"What was this place for?" I asked.

"Mr. Salisbury is settin' up a work shop, gonna put us all to work."

"Doing what?"

"Said he was setting up a lab, said we'd be lab assistants, you know technical work and sech."

"Lab work, huh?"

"You'd have to ask Mr. Salisbury, we didn't get into

133

the details."

"The more I know, the better chance I have of finding him."

"He tole us there'd be plenty of work in a week or so, asked me line up some of the boys. He's always good to us, real good. I shore hope nothin' happened to him." He smiled. "I was just havin' fun with you 'bout ole Tiberius."

TWENTY

Late afternoon back at the marina after a harrowing drive back from the Everglades. I was feeling less car sick and had just popped open a Budweiser when I noticed someone moving aboard Cameron's boat. The companionway hatch slid open and out came Donny, carrying the dog. The dog was trying to get away.

The lock on the hatch had been cut with bolt cutters. The bolt cutters were on the floor of the cockpit. He saw me approaching.

"I don't want trouble," he said, "what's mine is mine."

"If you don't want trouble leave the dog and go."

"I have as much right to that mutt as she does," he said.

"That sounds like a question for the police."

"See, here's what you don't understand. We don't need the police, you just need to mind your business."

Siegfried struggled in Donny's arms, his hands were so big he had trouble holding on to the little dog.   He was trying to climb over the rail onto the dock but it wasn't easy with his arms holding the dog.

He looked up at me. "I appreciate your concern, really I do, you're watching the neighborhood. But it's my dog and I'm taking it. End of conversation."

"I don't even think the dog wants to go with you."

"He'll come."

"Why don't you get off the boat and make arrangements -"

"Hey, know what? Now I'm getting pissed off. Why don't you mind your own fucking business?"

135

"I'm making this my business," I said.

"Tough guy, huh?"

Siegfried kicked free and darted back into the cabin. Donny followed. There was a Boston Whaler tied up alongside Cameron's boat, and I guessed whose it was. I uncleated the motorboat's bowline and dropped it in the water. The current was moving quickly. A few moments later Donny reappeared. He had a firm grip on Siegfried, his hairy forearm immobilizing the dog against his chest.

"Is that your boat?" I asked. I really hoped it was, as it had already drifted about twenty yards in the direction of the neighbor's stone jetty.

"The fuck?"

Donny scanned the thick vegetation on the shoreline between the dock and the stone jetty and obviously realized he could never get to the jetty before the boat did.

"Better leave the dog," I suggested.

He handed me Siegfried and dove, fully clothed, into the water. I watched him swim toward the drifting powerboat. He had to swim fast to catch it. But he had an athletic stroke and it wasn't too difficult, not after he kicked his shoes off.

He climbed up on the swim platform on the stern, dripping wet. He looked angry as he started the engine, and swung the boat around and gunned it toward me before suddenly veering away and heading out the channel. He left a wake that caused the boats in the marina to heave up and down. He yelled something too, but I couldn't make it out over the roar of the engine. I had a pretty good idea what the gist of it was.

I carried Siegfried aboard Hobo and gave him a cold hot dog, which he enjoyed. A few minutes later Cameron returned.

136

"Did he get out?" she asked.

"Not exactly."

"What happened?"

"Donny tried to take him."

"Are you kidding me?"

"I think he's really angry now."

"Angry? He's psychotic."

"I noticed."

She sighed. "Boy, I really know how to pick 'em."

Cameron and I drove to the hardware store where we bought a new padlock, one that was heavier than the last one. When we returned I fitted the lock on the clasp.

"I suggest you bring the dog with you wherever you go, and if they don't allow dogs, don't go there. Meanwhile, I'll talk to the guys at the front gate and make sure they know not to let Donny in. I don't want him schmoozing his way through. If he decides to return in the whaler I guess there's not much we can do. I may rig some trip wire tonight."

"I don't know what I'd do without you," she said.

"You would have managed."

"I'm not so sure. And I'm worried about you too. Donny doesn't give up. That's why he was so good at sacking quarterbacks."

TWENTY-ONE

Uncle Morris sat in his study and examined the object I had pocketed over at Salisbury's workshop. He turned it over in his hands.

"Where'd you find it?" he asked.

"Evan Salisbury built a building in the middle of nowhere off the Tamiami Trail. There were all kinds of chemicals, plus a bunch of rocks like these."

"What do you think it is?" he asked.

"I was hoping you might know."

He held the object close to his glasses. "Well, it's metal. This is ferric oxide."

"Come again?"

Uncle Morris looked up at me. "Rust."

He picked up a letter opener and began scraping one edge of the object. Something flaked off, revealing the material below it. He rubbed it with his hand.

"Huh," he said.

"What's huh?"

"Looks like silver, silver sulfide, to be precise."

"Silver?"

"Could be old coins he picked up somewhere. Whatever it is, it needs restoration."

"Like old Spanish coins?"

"Maybe. If it is, there should be markings, but we can't keep working on it with the knife. This whole mess needs to soak. I know a guy, owns an antique shop, name's Claude Baptiste. He does this sort of stuff. Funny guy, knows his way around. I think we should see him."

Baptiste worked in an old industrial brick building in the Design District. There was an antique shop in front. It was more of a junk shop selling old furniture, used crockery and brik-a-brak. Behind a glass display case of costume jewelry an elderly woman sat. She was working on a book of Soduko puzzles.

"Claude around?" asked Uncle Mo.

She nodded and pressed the button on an old-fashioned plastic intercom on her table.

"Claude, can you hear me?"

We waited for an answer.

"Yeah ma, what is it?"

"You got company."

Long pause.

"Ma, you gotta press the button all the way."

She rolled her eyes and pressed down with a long polished nail, careful not to break the nail.

"You got company."

"Who is it?"

"I don't know."

"Ma, you gotta press the button."

"I said I don't know."

"Well, can you ask him?"

"Wants to know who it is?"

"Tell him Morris Marsh."

Presently a thin man with a pale complexion and hollow eyes came in from the back room. He was wearing a dirty blue smock and struck me as the sort of person who would be discrete because he didn't talk to anyone anyway.

He led us down a hall to a cluttered workroom, with big tables and various jobs in progress. Model ships were being assembled and painted, no doubt to be sold in the shop, and there were several pieces of furniture under

139

repair. The room smelled strongly of paints and solvents. Against the far wall was a long counter, and on top of it a big rectangular glass tank filled with water.

"May I see it?" he asked, his voice almost a whisper.

"What?"

"Show him the rock," said Uncle Mo.

I lifted my plastic grocery bag onto a table and took out the rock. He examined it while I moseyed over to the watery contraption on the counter. There were tubes and pumps running into it, and wires strung across the top. From the wires, blackened coins, attached to metal clips, dangled in the fizzing water.

"Please don't touch anything," Claude said, without looking up.

There was a car battery by the side of the tank. It was wired to a metal rod submerged at one end of the tank. A similar rod attached to a metal plate was placed at the opposite end.

"What's in it, water?" I asked.

"It's a solution of ten percent sodium hydroxide, and yes, good old H2O, plus a few of my own secret ingredients."

"Sodium hydroxide?"

"It's basically an electrode reduction process, heard of it?" Claude asked.

"No, not really, so this is pretty common with guys who do what you do?"

"It's… pretty standard."

"You do a lot of this sort of thing?" I asked.

"Enough."

"There are a lot of guys like you?"

"A few, mostly at the universities, not exactly rocket science, provided you know what you're doing."

"I wouldn't think there'd be much call for this sort of thing."

He looked up at me. "The Spanish sent convoys loaded with goodies twice a year every year for 300 years. A lot of those ships sank. You do the math, so yeah, there's work for guys like me. You thought this is silver?" he asked.

"We just wondered."

"Where was it found?"

"We're not sure. Probably somewhere in the area," I said.

He looked at me without saying anything, then nodded. "I'll give it a try. I'll remove as much organic matter as possible, then I'll put it in the tank to remove the left-over deposits."

"Then what?" I asked.

"Then we'll wait."

"How long?"

He sighed. "Everyone wants everything right away, only that's not how it works. It depends how much corrosion, where it rested all this time on the ocean floor in relation to other metals, plus a lot of other factors."

"What kinda ballpark are we talking?"

"Two or three days at the earliest."

TWENTY-TWO

It had been a long day and I was happy to be back aboard Hobo where I felt safe, where I wasn't constantly looking for would-be assassins. There was no sign of Donny, and everything was quiet. I peeled off the Velcro straps on my bulletproof vest and let it drop to the cabin floor, my undershirt drenched in sweat. The air conditioner hummed on low, and the cabin was a cool relief. I was mixing myself a drink when through the porthole I glimpsed the bare ankles of a woman on deck. I guess I wasn't so safe after all. Virginia crept cat-like down the ladder. She was wearing a bikini bottom and a T-shirt with her belly showing.

"How about a drink?" I asked.

"Okay. Have you been swimming?"

She shook her head. "I've been waiting all afternoon and wondering where on Earth you could be. My imagination was running wild."

"Now, why would it do that?"

"Because I'm a bad girl."

"You are a bad girl, but people can change."

"Speak for yourself. What's done can't be undone."

Her fingers now clenched my shirt.

"Ted and Jane had to go to Tallahassee for the rest of the week and left me all alone."

"And you don't like to be alone."

She shook her head.

"You didn't want to go with them?"

"I didn't want to be a third wheel. Besides, I thought I

might enjoy some time alone."

She smiled and put her face close to me, her fingers crawled up my shirt.

"You're all hot. That was very impressive, how you got rid of that man earlier."

"Thanks, I thought so."

"Do you think he'll be back?"

"Probably."

"Which reminds me, while you were gone two men were looking for you."

I pushed her away. "Looking for me?"

"Uh huh."

"Who were they?"

"They didn't say."

"You spoke to them?"

"Just for a second. They left when I told them you weren't here."

"Who were they?"

"I told you, I don't know."

"Well what did they look like?"

"I dunno."

"This is important. Did they look foreign?"

"How would I know? Relax, you're getting all tense."

"I don't want to relax. I need to know who was here."

Virginia took a deep breath. "Two men, like I told you."

"Who looked like what?"

"I don't know. They were wearing long pants, kinda big guys, and T-shirts and gold chains. One of them was kinda fat."

"Kinda fat, okay, what else? Age, height, tattoos, identifying marks, hair color?"

Her eyes narrowed and scrunched up her nose. "No

143

tattoos, none that I could see. I guess they were about your age. They were suntanned, so they looked like they were from here. I already told you what they were wearing. Oh yeah, one of them had on a lot of cologne, and they both had real hairy arms."

"Real hairy arms, that's good. What else?"

"Uh, dark hair, I think. Well one had dark hair, the other I don't remember. Not long hair, just normal. One of them kinda looked like a boxer, you know, like he'd been beat up a few times. He had a crooked nose."

"That's it?"

"What do you want, a police sketch?"

"What did they say?" I asked.

"They said, 'we're looking for Harry McCoy.'"

"How'd they sound?"

"What do you mean?"

"Did they have a Russian accent?"

"Oh, uh, not really. Maybe."

"You're not sure?"

"I don't remember."

"They say anything else?"

"They said they'd try back."

"Jesus."

"Harry, if they came to hurt you, I hardly think they would have told me they'd be back."

"That's true." I sat on the settee. Suddenly I felt tired, and was starting to have a headache. Virginia began massaging my shoulders, rubbing against me.

"Listen Virginia, I don't think this is such a good idea. It's been a long day and I've got an early day tomorrow."

She stared at me for moment.

"So you're not interested in me anymore?"

I shook my head. "It's not that."

"What is it, then?"

"Look, I have a lot on my mind, and you do have a husband in Atlanta."

"Yeah, in Atlanta, and we're getting a divorce."

"But you're still legally married."

"What does that mean?"

"I'm sorry, it's just that I'm dealing with some serious issues."

"That's for sure."

"I think it would be better if this cooled off a little."

"You're an asshole, you know that?"

She turned and climbed out of the cabin. I let her go.

I sat on my bunk and took a deep breath. I wasn't sure who the foreign characters were who had come to the marina looking for me. To play it safe, I placed the 9 mm within easy reach, then I mixed myself a whisky and soda. I had another whisky and then another until I probably couldn't have shot straight anyway, and then I fell asleep.

Hours later, I jolted awake to the sound of grinding metal. It was coming from the air conditioner which was shaking and blowing hot air. I switched it off and opened all the portholes and hatches and found a warmish Coke in the iceless ice box and drank it. It was already sweltering hot, and pointless to try to go back to sleep. I turned on the early news: the new storm, Henrietta was on its way. Gus had turned into a tropical disturbance and steered west, kicking up high seas off the Yucatan. You wouldn't have known it from where I was -- the air hung hot and still. Before 6 a.m. I was showered and dressed. I threw on an FBI academy T-shirt and fished out a small canvas briefcase where I kept the boat papers. I emptied the papers and put the pistol in the briefcase. I put my second pistol, the Ruger sub-compact, in its holster and snapped it to my belt under my shirt in the small of my back. It was too hot for bulletproof vests, shoulder holsters and safari jackets.

After that I hoisted the faulty cooling device from the boat to the dock and manhandled it into the back seat of the Rabbit.

Doormen on the day shift were taking their places in front of the big hotels that lined Fountain Avenue, but it was still quiet. Traffic was light. A maintenance worker in a light blue uniform was hosing down the sidewalk in front of the Dolphin Hotel when I arrived. I parked the car and was the first customer at the coffee shop in the basement where I picked up a copy of the paper and sat at the counter. I read the newspaper and drank coffee while I waited for the rest of the world to wake up.

When I was finished with breakfast I walked out of the hotel lobby and started across the parking lot to my car. A white Mercedes pulled in front of me and stopped. From the front passenger seat out stepped a beefy looking guy in a tan suit and dark glasses.

"Harry McCoy?"

"Who's asking?"

"Juri Epstein wants to see you. I'm to bring you."

"Maybe some other time."

"He said I'm to bring you."

The door to the back seat opened and a second man stepped out. He was dressed in long trousers, fancy lizard skin loafers and a silky-looking shirt, and held a pistol which he discretely aimed at my chest.

"We don't want no trouble," he said.

The man in the suit took my briefcase. "You'll get this back later," he said. "Get in."

I did as I was told. I didn't have much choice. In the backseat, which was upholstered in leather, the man in the

146

lizard shoes patted me down as the driver pulled away. He missed the gun, excellent candidate for the TSA.

"Where are we going?" I asked.

"Not far."

"Does your boss always arrange meetings like this? Didn't he ever hear of e-mail, or maybe sending a text message?"

No answer.

"This isn't about Demetri Popov, is it? Say, you guys ever hear of his cousin, guy named Junior?" I was met with silence. "You guys don't talk much, do you?"

Fifteen minutes later we were in front of a bar in North Miami called The Bay Club.

A muscular fellow in a tight black tennis shirt opened the door and I was shown in. I followed him through the empty club, out French doors onto a terra cotta patio that led to a yacht that was about four times the length of Hobo. It was the sort of yacht that has marble baths and discos on board. Probably a wine cellar too.

Juri Epstein was at an outdoor bar. He was wearing a loose fitting linen shirt and had graying hair and beard, cut short. He was talking on his cell phone, and ignored us. His entourage was positioned casually around the otherwise empty patio. Presently he issued something that sounded like an order in Russian and snapped the phone shut.

"Harry McCoy, I've heard a lot about you, finally we meet. Juri Epstein, thanks for coming in."

He said it like I'd had a choice in the matter.

"Have a seat. Can I get you something to drink? Coffee, juice?"

"Thanks, I'm fine." I sat at a bar stool next to Juri.

"You're probably wondering why I asked you here."

"It crossed my mind."

147

"I understand you've been having some... problems lately."

"Nothing I can't handle."

"Oh really?" He twisted his head and raised his eyebrow. "I hope so. But you see, these problems, they could also be a problem for me." He wiggled his hand in the air. "There are some people in town who give people like me a bad name."

"How do you mean?"

"How do I explain? See, not everyone understands the American way of doing business."

He looked at me to see if I understood. I didn't.

"Put another way, look at any successful businessman, like say, a Donald Trump. Perception, image are all very important."

"You're worried about your reputation?"

He snapped his fingers. "You're smart, you catch on quickly."

"I'm not sure I understand what that has to do with me."

"It has to do with you because you shot Demetri."

"Not until he tried to kill me first."

He smiled. "Of course, but you see, now everything's gotten stirred up."

"Blame it on Demetri, not me."

"True, and to be honest, you probably did me a favor."

"Oh, why's that?"

"He wasn't a very good employee."

"Depends on what his job was."

"The fact is I was going to fire him. Demetri liked to freelance, and that was a problem for me, because Demetri, well, he still did things the way we used to do things in Russia, if you see what I mean."

"I think I do."

"It draws negative publicity for the immigrant community."

"Yeah, and innocent people get killed."

"Tell me, why do you think someone would want to kill Evan Salisbury?" asked Juri.

I shook my head.

He smiled. "So we'd both like to know. I understand you've been receiving death threats."

"A few."

"I might be able to help you there."

"How would you do that?"

"Let's just say, I know how to pull strings here and there. I see an opportunity."

"How's that?"

"I help you with this Junior character, and you stop kicking up trouble for me in the Russian community."

"I've been hired to find Evan Salisbury. I intend to go where the investigation leads. If that causes bad PR for you, I really don't give a shit. For all I know, one of your goons here was with Demetri the night he murdered Andrew Bigelow."

Juri smiled.

"I don't have goons in my organization." He gestured to his entourage. "Do these guys look like goons to you? They don't look like goons to me." He pointed his index finger at me, his elbow resting on the bar. "I run legitimate businesses, and if you know what's good for you, you'll steer your investigation 180 degrees in the other direction. I'm prepared to double whatever your client is paying. You'll work for me. Like I said, I'm interested to find out what this is all about."

"And if I refuse?"

Epstein nodded to a large man seated by the bar. The man stood up.

"Liam will explain things, he's very good at explaining."

Liam, who had about a size 32 neck, stood up and smiled. He picked up a Miami yellow pages off the bar. He grasped it with both hands. He ripped it in half. I tried to look non-plussed. Then Epstein nodded and Liam sat down.

"Does he do any other tricks?" I asked.

"Consider that friendly advice. You don't know what you're up against. That can be a fatal mistake. Think about it, Mr. McCoy."

TWENTY-THREE

Twenty minutes later they dropped me back at the hotel. Say what you will about Juri Epstein, the complimentary limo service was very thoughtful. I drove to the repair shop and dropped off the air conditioner, then returned to the marina. Lopez was waiting.

"You're not wearing the vest," he observed.

"Too hot, besides, it looks funny."

I told him about my meeting with Juri Epstein.

"He's got a guy who tears phone books in half?"

"Yep."

"And he offered to pay you to work for him?"

"Correct."

"What about the police, he paying them too?"

I shrugged. "He said he doesn't like the publicity. Said he doesn't like it that his guys are involved, but said he didn't have anything to do with it. I think he wants information, can't stand to be in the dark. That's my gut."

"You trust him?"

"I don't have to trust him."

Epstein's interest in me was partially explained ten minutes later. Lopez and I had just turned onto I-95 southbound toward Valerie Shoupe's house when my cell phone rang. It was Consuela. I put it on speaker.

"Can you come by the station?"

"Sure, why?"

"We picked up a guy named Aleksei Pederov. According to the file, he's a friend of Demetri's. We want

151

you to have a look at him. We think he might be the other shooter."

"What's he in for?"

"We have him on a weapons charge, at a nightclub last night. We won't be able to hold him for long, he's getting a lawyer."

"I'll be there in ten." I said.

"Odd coincidence," said Lopez.

I nodded.

"Must be why Epstein sent for you this morning. But what does it mean?"

"We'll find out. Maybe Juri's just like the rest of us, trying to find out what's going on before it blows up in his face."

"Maybe, and maybe he's trying to stop you from getting too close to something."

We made it to police headquarters ten minutes later. Consuela was waiting in the lobby. We followed her into the elevator and up to the floor where the interrogation room was. She led us into the adjacent room on the back side of a one-way mirror. We watched as the door to the interrogation room opened and a man was escorted in by a uniformed cop. He looked straight at the mirror and raised his middle finger. He smiled. He was wearing a silk Versace shirt, Italian shoes and a large diamond and gold ring on his finger. I thought he looked like a Ukrainian pimp, or what I imagined one would look like.

Consuela and I were standing behind the mirror.

"Something tells me he's been through this before," I said.

"Recognize him?"

I studied him through the mirror. Pederov slouched in

his chair, legs sprawled, elbows on the armrests.

"Can't say for sure," I said.

A man in a tan poplin suit and bowtie entered and stood next to Consuela. He carried a thick brown cardboard file folder and also juggled a cup of coffee. I guessed he was from the DA's office. He sat down and got his papers and coffee situated. "So who is this bozo?" the man asked.

"Salisbury shooting suspect, one of Demetri's pals," said Consuela. "Picked him up on a weapons charge early this morning. Goes by the name of Aleksei Pederov. We're hoping Harry here might recognize him. We thought maybe he could be one of the guys who tried to kill Evan Salisbury."

The man looked me over. "And is he?"

"It was dark," I said.

"Usually is at night," said the man in the suit, sipping his coffee.

"I can't be sure."

After letting Pederov stew for a few minutes, Muldoon entered the interrogation room. Pederov eyed him with a look of bemusement. It was an arrogance I had seen before in hoods who knew the ropes, hoods who were just plain stupid, and hoods who had good lawyers. I wasn't sure which category he belonged to.

Muldoon was followed by another man who shook hands in a perfunctory way with Pederov.

"His lawyer?" I asked.

Consuela nodded.

"That was fast."

The lawyer wore a Prince of Wales plaid suit, double breasted with peaked lapels. He had a white silk hankie in the pocket.

"My client agrees to answer questions but reserves his

rights," said the lawyer.

Pederov shrugged. "I don't need lawyer."

"Shut up," said the lawyer.

"I don't do nothing wrong."

Muldoon started. "For the record, where were you Sunday night, around 1 a.m.?"

Pederov looked at his attorney, who nodded.

"Probably I'm sleeping."

The lawyer interrupted. "My client has stated that he was in his residence in South Beach."

"Can anyone corroborate that?"

"Not at this time," the lawyer answered.

"And where are you employed, Mr. Pederov?"

Pederov looked at his lawyer. The lawyer nodded again.

"I work in gym."

"Biscayne Health Club and Spa?"

"Yeah."

"And what do you do there, Mr. Pederov?"

"I'm personal trainer."

Muldoon took a moment to scrutinize Pederov's gold watch and silk shirt.

"What was your relationship with Demetri Popov?" Muldoon's questioning was workmanlike. He looked directly at Pederov. He was watching his eyes. A good interrogator can tell if a man is lying by looking at his eyes. When someone is making something up his eyes shift left, when they're trying to remember something, they shift right, or maybe it was the other way around. I never could remember.

"He's my friend, everybody know."

"Problem is, your friend was killed while perpetrating a crime, a very serious crime. Since you were so close, that doesn't make things look too good for you."

"I think maybe Demetri a little crazy."

"When was the last time you saw Demetri?"

Pederov looked at his lawyer. The lawyer nodded.

"I don't remember."

"Try."

"Maybe five days ago, at gym."

"Friday?"

"Yeah, okay maybe."

"Are you familiar with the penalty for perjury?"

Before Pederov could answer Muldoon began reciting the penal code. A good performance, but Pederov registered no emotion.

Pederov's lawyer looked at his watch. "I think that just about does it." He snapped his briefcase shut. "Will that be all?"

"Yeah, for now."

I turned to Consuela. "You're letting him walk?"

"We don't have enough to hold him. That's why I wanted you here."

"At least hold him 36 hours, soften him up."

The man in the poplin suit shook his head. "A deal's a deal. This one's coming from upstairs."

"You're just letting him go?" I asked.

"You got a problem talk to Lt. Halloran. We've got no evidence to hold him, just the misdemeanor gun possession. Best we can do is have his visa revoked and deport him. Other than that, there's not much we can do, you know that and I know that," said Consuela.

"And now he does too."

TWENTY-FOUR

Pederov had a smirk on his face as he left the police station. He was met at the curb by a man chewing a toothpick and leaning against the hood of a blue BMW 5 Series. Pederov got into the passenger side of the front seat while the other man drove. Lopez and I followed in Lopez's car as they drove north to 36th Street, then turned east and crossed the Julia Tuttle Causeway to Miami Beach. The car pulled over on Collins Avenue where Pederov got out in front of a strip club called Heat Wave. It had a black awning with a gold flame and a woman's silhouette painted on it. We parked across the street.

"Now what?" asked Lopez.

"I don't know. We wait, I guess."

"That's 90 percent of what I do. You think this guy was with Demetri when they tried to kill Salisbury?"

"Could be, but it was too dark, I can't be sure. When he comes back out we'll follow him."

"You think he might still be working for Epstein?"

I shrugged. "He might lead us to whoever put out the hit on Salisbury."

Forty-five minutes passed and my stomach was growling. I got out of the car and found a deli not too far from the strip club. I bought two bottles of water and two turkey subs and returned to the car.

"Anything?" I asked.

Lopez shook his head. We ate the sandwiches. The windows were rolled down but the inside of the car was sweltering.

"You think he's still in there?" asked Lopez, wiping his mouth with a paper napkin. "I just hope there isn't a back door. He could be screwing with us."

"One way to find out. I'll go look."

"You don't think he'll recognize you?"

I was wearing a New York Mets baseball cap, which I pulled down. "If he comes out follow him."

I got out of the car and went into the strip club.

Heat Wave didn't attract what would be described as an upscale clientele. The lunch crowd was mostly middle-aged overweight men who had given up on meeting women other than those who performed lap dances for money. There were a few dozen small round tables arranged in front of a small stage. There was a bar on one side and the place was very dark. On the stage there was a pole. A girl without a top was dancing. She wasn't very good, kept slipping off the pole. She didn't have the arm or abdominal muscles required, but the men who were watching her didn't seem to mind. The girl didn't seem to mind either, she was just going through the motions. Then again it was 2 p.m., maybe she saved her best moves for the evening performance.

I noticed light coming from behind a curtained doorway near the stage. I walked over to the bar and ordered a Budweiser. After a few minutes I heard voices, a man with a Russian accent. I glanced behind the curtain. A dingy hallway led to a men's room, and a back office. The door to the office was ajar. I crept down the hall. Through the open door, I caught a glimpse of a man dipping his pinky into a plastic bag, then snorting white powder from his fingernail. Pederov was counting a small stack of bills.

I returned to the car. At about 3 o'clock Pederov finally

157

emerged. He squinted at the bright light, then put on a pair of shades. He walked east. I followed on foot, Lopez kept well back in the car. Pederov walked three blocks and turned left on Collins and went into a massage parlor called Serenity Spa. Lopez parked half a block past it. I put on a pair of sunglasses and the baseball cap and followed him in. There was a small reception room, dimly lit, with mismatched office chairs arranged around the perimeter. Soothing Chinese string music played. There was a hallway leading off the waiting room, separated by a beaded curtain.

There were no customers in the waiting room. A sullen Asian woman in her mid-twenties wearing a tank top sat on a stool behind a cash register. I pulled a fifty out of my wallet and placed it on the counter.

"I'll take whatever that'll get me."

"Fifty dollar, nice massage." She said in a loud flat voice. "Follow me."

There were five doors in the hallway. Three of them, including the one I entered, were ajar. The room was small, with a massage table and a small cupboard. The walls were flimsy fake wood paneling. A Chinese calendar on a bamboo scroll was the only decoration.

"Someone be right here," she said, and handed me a skimpy pale blue cotton robe, then she left the room, closing the door behind her. I tossed the robe onto the massage table and waited with my ear to the door until I heard her pass through the beaded curtain. I went into the hall. There were two closed doors. I picked one and opened it. A bald man in black socks, not Pederov, was lying on the table while a plump Chinese woman straddled him, her hands on his chest.

"Sorry, wrong room," I said.

158

I shut the door and turned to the next, pulling my pistol from the clip at the back of my belt.

Pederov lay face up on the massage table, waiting for his masseuse. There was a small towel draped over his midsection. His eyes were closed.

"What took you so long?" he asked.

I placed the blued steel barrel of the Glock under the tip of his nose.

"We're conducting a customer service survey. It'll only take a few minutes." He opened his mouth to object, and I slid the oiled barrel of the pistol into his mouth.

His eyes opened wide, he looked like someone in the dentist's chair.

"First question: did someone put a contract out on Evan Salisbury?"

He tried to talk, but gagged on the gun. I took it out of his mouth.

"Fuck you."

I shoved the barrel of the gun deeper into his mouth until he gagged. Then I pulled it out.

"Let's try this again."

"You're crazy."

"I'm not going to ask again. Who told Demetri to hit Salisbury? Was it Juri Epstein?"

He shook his head. "Epstein didn't have anything to do with it."

"Who then?"

"I don't know."

"But you know it wasn't Epstein."

"Demetri was working for someone else, I don't know who."

He started to sit up. I pressed his back. He reached for the pistol and the next thing I knew we were wrestling for it. I saw a plastic bottle of oil and grabbed it. I squirted it in his face. He let go of the Glock and started wiping his eyes. I put the barrel of the pistol behind his neck. The veins in his neck were bulging and he was breathing heavily.

"Question number two: who put the contract out on me?"

"Demetri's cousin, Junior. He say he want you dead. He say anybody who kill you he gonna take care of."

"Does that include you? That why you were carrying?"

"I got a license to carry."

"Not an unregistered weapon, you don't."

"What, you gonna bust my balls for chicken shit?"

"Who else wants me dead?"

"Lotsa people. You ain't gonna last the week."

"You don't think so?"

"I might kill you myself."

"Tough guy, huh? Okay, getting back to my earlier question, who wanted Salisbury dead?"

Pederov was sweating.

"I only know there's a guy, Mink, he talk to Demetri, he give Demetri money, say there will be more when job is done. Demetri, he don't ask no questions."

"Mink?"

"Yeah."

"How much?"

"Ten thousand."

"Mink lived in a trailer park, where would he get ten thousand dollars, and why would he want Salisbury dead?"

"I don't know. Nobody know."

I looked at Pederov's face, trying to decide if he knew more than he was letting on. I figured I didn't have much time before whatever they had in the way of security

160

showed up.

"Who was with Demetri the night he murdered the kid?"

Pederov hesitated.

"Was it Junior?"

"Maybe."

"Where do I find him?"

I pressed harder, the pistol caused him to bend his neck. He grimaced in pain.

"Okay, okay, I know he got a girlfriend, Arina."

"Where do I find her?"

"She work at a restaurant, steak place, Le Viande, something like that."

"Where does she live?"

"I told you plenty."

I supposed he had. "Okay, we'll leave it at that, and no one needs to know about our little conversation. Understood?"

The door opened and a tall woman with a sallow complexion entered. She was holding a towel and a bottle of body oil. She stopped in the doorway.

"Sorry about the mess," I said.

TWENTY-FIVE

The next morning I phoned Valerie to give her a status report. She sounded like she was still a satisfied client, and asked that I come by later to deliver my next report in person. At around 11 a.m. Lopez and I initiated a stake-out at the restaurant where Junior's girlfriend, Arina, worked. I liked that, "initiated a stake-out." It sounded very professional. I would have to use that in my report.

Le Viande was a small bistro in Coral Gables. Lopez parked close enough so we could see, but far enough away so we probably wouldn't be noticed. The street was lined with small apartment buildings. There was a coffee shop on the corner, with a catalpa tree in front. We were parked under the tree.

Lopez killed the engine. We rolled down the windows and hot air wafted in. I got out of the car and walked past the restaurant. It served lunch and dinner, but hadn't opened for lunch yet. Inside there was a waiter in black pants, white oxford shirt and a white apron. He was setting up the tables, and a bartender was stocking the bar. I couldn't see anyone else, so I returned to the car.

Nothing happened for the next half hour except a mailman in Bermuda shorts and a pith helmet delivered the mail, and a calico cat walked slowly across the street and entered the coffee shop. Lopez chewed on a toothpick, one elbow out the open window, a foot on the dashboard.

"You think Pederov tipped her off?" he asked.

"Why tell us about her if he was going to tip her off?"

"So he would look like he was cooperating, or set us up

162

in a trap?"

I shrugged. "Who knows?"

We sat quietly for about ten minutes, watching. Lopez shifted in his seat, as if figuring out how to say something.

"What is it?" I asked.

"I was just thinking what I'd do if I was Evan Salisbury and I was on the run."

"Yes?"

"I guess it would depend on why someone tried to kill me. But if there were a hit out on me, and for whatever reason I couldn't call the cops, I'd get as much cash together as I could and skip the country. Maybe the islands. Guy like Salisbury probably has lots of money in an offshore account, maybe even a private plane. That's what I'd do."

"Makes sense. More coffee?"

He shook his head.

We watched as a Toyota Rav 4 pulled up near the restaurant and a petite woman with dark hair got out. She went into the restaurant. A little while later Lopez got out of the car and walked past the restaurant. When he got back he said the woman was waiting on tables. She was the only waitress in the place.

This was the part about being a detective that's not so glamorous. More waiting. In Le Viande I imagined they were eating entrecote steaks with pommes frites and mustard sauce. I was chewing on a Italian sub with wilted lettuce and a mushy tomato I'd purchased at a gas station.

Two hours into it. Lopez slouched in his seat. His foot jiggled back and forth, and he rhythmically folded and refolded his plastic coffee stirrer.

"I got borderline high blood pressure, the doctor says my job is too stressful. So he wants me cut down on the coffee," he said.

163

"Maybe you shouldn't listen to your doctor."

"Maybe."

He put the plastic stirrer in his mouth and chewed it for a while.

"So you never been married?" asked Lopez.

I shook my head. "You?"

"Nah."

"Let me ask you something, tell me if it's too personal."

"Shoot."

"Why the gig as a security guard? In a town like this, you must have a pretty steady clientele as a P.I."

"Rent-a-cop, right?"

I nodded.

"I just don't like waiting for work when it gets slow, so I call my friend at the agency, and he hooks me up."

"Makes sense."

"What about you?" he asked.

"What about me?"

"How'd you end up in this game? Lawyer and all."

"It fell into my lap, I figure maybe it was meant to be, maybe I'd be good at it."

Lopez nodded, as if that made sense too.

The sky turned darker and then the rain came. Water beaded under the saturated canvas top and dripped through a tiny tear Lopez had tried to mend with black duct tape. At about 3 o'clock, Arina, or the woman we thought might be Arina, left the restaurant. She was struggling with a bent umbrella which wasn't enough in the heavy downpour. We watched as the umbrella blew out while she was unlocking the car, and she got soaked.

We followed her north on Coral Way. She turned into an apartment complex and we watched as she parked her car and dashed up some stairs to a second floor apartment with an entrance on the balcony. We left her there. It was getting late so we decided to work in shifts.   Lopez dropped me off at the marina garage. I picked up my car and returned to the stake-out alone. By the time I got to her apartment what was left of the sun had come out again.

I figured Arina might be awhile, maybe she was resting between shifts, and would return to the restaurant for dinner. Maybe Junior would pay his girlfriend a visit. At about 4 o'clock she emerged from her apartment and headed north. I followed.

She turned onto I-95 and then exited in the warehouse district in Lemon City, a Haitian neighborhood just north of the airport. A historical marker I passed identified it as an old part of town, but there wasn't much left from old Miami that I could tell, except an old church, weathered by years of tropical air. She pulled up in front of a small warehouse and got out of the car.

Arina knocked on the steel door to a warehouse office. There was an air conditioner mounted above the door, the windows were protected by metal grates. A moment later the door opened and a heavy-set man appeared. He had big round shoulders and meaty arms that hung straight down like an ape's.

Arina went into the office and came back out a few minutes later and drove away, I followed her back to the restaurant. I figured she was there for the dinner service, so I returned to the warehouse.

The office was part of a warehouse for a company called Caribbean International. In back was a paved lot that took up half the block and was surrounded by an 8-foot chain link fence. On top of the fence were three stands of razor wire. Discarded plastic grocery bags and sheets of newspaper were caught in the razor wire.   The grass

165

margin around the fence was uncut and littered with rubbish. Up the block was a check cashing place with a hand-lettered sign on the wall, "checks cashed, lottery tickets." A few men loitered out front in mismatched plastic chairs. Other than that, the neighborhood was deserted.

I texted Lopez.

"At Carib Int'l warehouse SE 40 Lemon City. Arina here will check out"

He texted back.

"OK, I'm back at Heat Wave. Pederov here"

"Gr8"

"Ok if I expense drink and gratuity?"

"Of course!"

"Lap dance? Haha"

"Go 4 it."

Then I pulled on my baseball cap and waited. At 5 o'clock workers started to punch out. I watched from across the street until the last one left the office, locking the door behind him.

Scaling the fence would have been easy enough. Getting over the razor wire, not so easy. I walked around the perimeter of the property until I got to the neighboring business, a lumberyard. The gate was open. I walked through the yard until I came to an interior fence, without razor wire, dividing the two businesses. Against the fence there was a stack of pressure-treated 2 x 4's which I climbed on top of. From there I could reach the top of the fence. No one was looking so I pulled myself over and dropped onto the other side.

I stood still for a moment, watching and listening for a night watchman, or, more my luck, an attack dog, but the place was deserted. Someone had left a small pry bar on the ground where crates were being broken down. I picked it up and slipped it into my pocket.

Caribbean International's lot contained a dumpster and a dozen or so shipping containers, 20- and 40-footers. Some of them were new, others old, rusty, and derelict. More coming in than going out. Several others were placed on trailers, waiting to be hauled away. The containers were padlocked. I walked over to the warehouse and looked through a dirty window on the back door. I could see brand new furniture wrapped in plastic and boxes of electronics and other stuff that looked to be from an expensive shopping trip, ready for shipment to the islands. I gathered Caribbean International handled the shipping.

The door to the warehouse was wooden, and old, and easy to open with the pry bar, the dry wood near the bolt breaking easily. I moved quickly through the warehouse to the office. It was furnished with an old steel desk and filing cabinets and smelled of dust and stale coffee.

On the desk were shipping documents, a calendar with half dressed women posing around a truck and a menu from a Chinese restaurant.

There was a bulletin board near a small kitchenette. A note was pinned to it, whoever worked in the office was efficient, but not a great speller. "Atten – all drivers, Everybody has to have there license. We need copies on file – for insurance. Plus fill out the form or you cant do delivaries. Please leave in basket. This means you! No exeptions."

I noticed a basket on top of the filing cabinet. In it were Xeroxed copies of drivers' licenses, and forms with information about driving records. Switching on the desk lamp, I leafed through the papers. I got half way through the stack, not sure what I was looking for, when I stopped.

It was a copy of a driver's license, and it belonged to Clifford Mink.

So Pederov had told me the truth, Mink was mixed up in this, connected to Demetri, somehow. I was mulling over the meaning of that when I heard voices in the yard. I quickly turned off the lamp and was very still, listening. When I didn't hear anything, I tried the steel door leading to the sidewalk, but it wouldn't open. The bolt needed a key on the inside. I cursed to myself and backtracked through the darkened warehouse to the backdoor, where I listened quietly, motionless in the shadows. Slowly, I pushed the door open.

I stepped into the yard, closed the door behind me, and hurried toward the fence where I had climbed over. As I turned the corner around a rusted container, there, standing in front of me, were two men dressed in work clothes. One of them had something in his hand. As I started to speak - I had in mind something about looking for the bathroom - I saw that the object in his hand was a Tazer. His finger pressed on the trigger and a wire shot toward me. The jolt of electricity knocked me to the ground.

It was like having a seizure. A very painful seizure. I tried to talk but couldn't, and had a vague sensation of being carried somewhere, and then a metal gate slamming shut, and then I passed out.

When I came to I was lying in the dark in a place where the air was fetid and thick. I moved my head and felt a wave of pain and nausea. I closed my eyes and swallowed hard, then slowly opened my eyes and let them adjust to the darkness. There were pinpricks of light above and I sat up. My forehead smashed into a steel ceiling. I collapsed onto my back. I felt with my hands, realizing, to my horror, that I was inside one of the shipping containers. I was lying on top of a palletized stack of boxes, banded together and covered in heavy plastic sheeting.

I closed my eyes. Then I patted my pockets, but my cell phone was gone. Not good.

There was about 18 inches between the top layer of boxes and the ceiling. At one end of the container I could see a sliver of light where the door was. I slowly slid toward the door and tried kicking it open. It didn't budge. As my eyes adjusted further to the dimness, I saw that the bolt securing the door to the top of the frame was nearly an inch of hardened steel. Any latch, if there was one on the inside, was blocked by the tightly stacked boxes.

I reached into my pocket and removed a small pocket knife and began cutting the plastic bands and shrink wrap that covered the pallets. I ripped open the top box. It was a case of liquor. I got rid of the bottles by slinging them to the back of the container, where some of them smashed, and soon the smell of whisky filled the container. When the box was empty I pulled it out and began working on the next box, so after about twenty minutes I had created a space large enough for me to stand. I removed more boxes, sliding them to the back of the container. After I had removed a dozen or so cartons in this manner, I now had room to open the door's clasp. My clothes and hair were soaked in sweat, and coated in dust and dirt. I pulled on the clasp, but the door would not open.

I pounded my fist against the door in frustration, then screamed like a man in an insane asylum, the sound reverberating off the walls of the container. And when I was done, I lay down on the cartons and kicked the walls of my prison box until I didn't have any kick left in me. The air was thick and foul, and eventually I passed out.

I came to as the latch was being unlocked from the outside. The gate opened, flooding the container with early evening light. I grabbed a bottle and prepared to defend myself.

"Whoa, take it easy."

Gradually my eyes adjusted to the bright light and the figures before me came into focus - Lopez and Consuela.

"Jesus, Harry, you smell like a distillery," she said.

TWENTY-SIX

"Good idea to smash the bottles of booze, we didn't have any trouble finding you. What the hell happened?" asked Consuela.

"Someone zapped me. Next thing I know I'm in the shipping container."

"You've got blood all over your head," observed Lopez.

"I hit my head on the ceiling. What happened to the Russian?"

"He started partying pretty hard at the club. Looked like he might stay awhile so I decided I better come back here. You weren't around so I phoned Detective Esperanza."

"So you guys don't think I can take care of myself?"

"A simple 'thank you' is okay," replied Consuela.

"Thank you."

"Don't mention it. Besides, Lt. Halloran said I should keep an eye on you."

"I didn't think we hit it off, now he wants you to help protect me?"

"Not exactly. He said if you want to get yourself killed that's your business, that as long as you're alive we stand a better chance of finding what happened to Evan Salisbury. After this, Harry, you can expect me to stick tight. For now, let's go to my house and we'll get you fixed up," she said.

Lopez drove, following Consuela toward her house.

"So what's the deal with Detective Esperanza?" he asked as he drove.

"What do you mean?"

"I mean, she's single right? No ring."

"I don't know."

"No ring, no husband, means she's available."

"She could have a boyfriend," I said.

He shook his head. "I don't think so."

"How do you know?"

"I asked a friend in the department."

"And?"

"He said she's not going with anyone." Lopez turned to me. "So she's available. You still seeing that lady at the marina, Virginia?"

"You're very observant, you know that? You ought to consider a career as a private detective."

"So how's it going with her?"

"That's over."

"Okay, just checking," he said.

We parked in front of Consuela's house. They got me settled in her living room and then went back for my car. When they returned Consuela strongly suggested I take a shower, after which I changed into the gym clothes I kept in the car. When I finished dressing I walked into the kitchen where I found Lopez deep in conversation with Consuela. She looked up.

"I better take a look at the cut on your head."

"I'll do it," said Lopez. "I had medical training in the army."

"It's no big deal, I have a first aid kit," said Consuela.

"I thought you were going to fix some drinks?" he said.

"You be the bartender," she replied.

"Okay," Lopez said, reluctantly. I sat down and Consuela started cleaning the cut on my head. She daubed a gauze with alcohol on my scalp.

"So what the hell happened?" she asked.

172

"We had a lead on Junior's girlfriend. Don't ask me how, you don't want to know."

"Yeah, it wasn't pretty," added Lopez from the kitchen.

"Anyway, we followed her to the warehouse. As soon as the place cleared out, I went in for a look."

"And you got jumped?" she asked.

"Basically."

"So they locked you up until they could get Junior."

"Probably."

"Good thing we found you."

"That's for sure. But at least we got a lead on Junior."

"Maybe," Consuela was examining the cut on my head. "Or maybe now he's going to be even harder to find. You probably spooked him, thank you very much. This doesn't look too bad, I don't think you need any stitches."

"Someone who works at the warehouse will know something," I said.

"Muldoon and I'll go over tomorrow, see what we can find out."

I sat straight up. "I forgot to mention, Clifford Mink was a driver for Caribbean International."

"Clifford Mink? My victim?"

I nodded.

"That's interesting," she said. "So Mink worked at Earl's Boatyard. He serviced Salisbury's boat, but he also worked part-time as a delivery driver?"

"Lady at the trailer park said he was a driver, too," said Lopez, carrying in the drinks from the bar. At first I thought they were shots of tequila, then I realized he had mixed lemon martinis.

Consuela took one of the drinks. "Which means he's the link. Mink put Demetri onto Evan, somehow, for whatever reason."

173

I nodded. "They hit Salisbury and maybe when the hit didn't go off they didn't want anyone talking."

"And someone whacks Mink," Lopez.

"But who put out the hit on Salisbury in the first place?" she asked. "Meanwhile Halloran thinks Salisbury is responsible for Bernie Leach's murder."

"Yeah? And who killed Andrew Bigelow? That doesn't make sense."

"I agree. I think Halloran's on the wrong track. I'll talk to him. Meanwhile, I think it would be a good idea if we continue sharing information on a daily basis, off the record."

I nodded. "So what do you know about Caribbean International?"

"I did a quick check earlier, import-export business, small consolidated shipments to the islands."

"Who owns it?"

"Records show the owner is Robert Simms, it's a legitimate business as far as we know. I'm guessing the employees are running a drug smuggling operation that the owner probably doesn't even know about. There's no link to Epstein. My guess is Junior's involved, and like I said, they put you on ice until Junior showed up."

We finished our martinis, and then had another round. When we were done I started to stand up, then felt a wave of dizziness. I sat back down.

Consuela looked concerned. "Are you all right, Harry?"

"Whoa."

"He's fine, I better drive him home," said Lopez.

"Maybe it would be better if you went on," said Consuela. "He can stay here, where I can keep an eye on him. I don't think he should be left alone."

"Yeah, not with a head injury," I said.

174

"I can watch him," said Lopez.

"It's just a little dizziness, probably nothing," I said.

Consuela looked concerned. "He should stay. I think this is best."

Consuela saw Lopez to the door, then returned to the couch.

"You just sent my ride home."

"Hmmm."

"Why'd you do that?"

"I already told you, I'm taking you into protective custody."

I was feeling drowsy. Consuela relaxed on the couch beside me.

"We never finished our conversation, from the other night. Will you tell me about your partner, Lucy Davenport?"

"Why?"

"Because I want to know," said Consuela.

"She died."

"What happened?"

I shook my head. "She was beautiful, and she's dead, and it was my fault, and that's all there is to tell."

"Someone's dead and there's nothing to tell?"

I took a deep breath and looked at my glass. It was empty. "I was in charge of an investigation, this was Jimmy Picolo, you probably heard of him."

She nodded.

"We had a witness who had offered to testify. I let Lucy handle him. She worked for me in the Investigative Division. Lucy was supposed to meet the witness in a restaurant in Brooklyn, talk to him, get him to come in. I should have sent a security detail. I should have gone myself. But I didn't, I screwed up, I let her go alone. Lucy

175

led one of Picolo's guys to my witness. He killed them both. Lucy was 28."

Consuela put her arm on my shoulder. "Harry, that's our business, things like that happen sometimes."

"Tell that to Lucy Davenport."

TWENTY-SEVEN

When I woke I was on the sofa covered with a thin cotton blanket. Consuela was standing over me. She was wearing a bright green blazer and slipping a slim Beretta 9mm into her shoulder holster. Despite the weapon, the jacket showed off her supple curves. The overall effect was very satisfactory.

"I let you sleep. How do you feel?"

"Better."

She smiled, then a look of concern crossed her face. "I'm nervous about leaving you."

"How about breakfast?"

"Gotta meet Muldoon."

"Oh, him."

She smiled. "He is my partner, you know."

"Can I at least buy you a cup of coffee?"

"I'm going to grab a cafe con leche at Versailles."

She pronounced it "Bersailles." I really liked the way she said it. It was a popular Cuban eatery on Calle Oche in Little Havana where they served take-out Cuban coffee.

I stood up, and put on a robe Consuela offered. It smelled of lemony perfume.

"What's this scent?"

"Eau Sauvage, it's Dior man's aftershave, if you must know."

"Oh, boyfriend?" I guess Lopez's source had bad information.

"Some women use it. I wear it as my perfume."

"Interesting."

"Harry, I've got to run. Will you lock the door? I phoned Esteban, he said he'd be right over."

"Esteban?"

"Steve? Lopez. Your partner?"

"Oh, right."

"There's OJ in the fridge, and muffins. You're sure you're all right?"

"I'm fine, and thanks."

I walked her to the door and watched as she climbed into her silver Audi TT. She drove away. Fast. Twenty minutes later Lopez picked me up. He was wearing dark wrap around glasses and a green and yellow soccer shirt. He didn't say much until we were in the car.

"So?"

I looked at him. "What?"

"You okay?"

"I'm fine."

"How'd it go after I left?"

"What do you mean?"

"Anything happen?"

"Like what?"

"I don't know."

"We chatted for a while, then I slept on the couch."

"What did you talk about?"

"This and that."

"Huh."

"Why?"

"No reason."

Lopez dropped me at the marina, then headed to do surveillance work at Earl's. We had agreed to keep working in shifts. It was a hunch, but I didn't want to take too much attention off other aspects of our investigation. I climbed aboard Hobo to check the boat and change into a pair of Madras shorts, blue tennis shirt and sneakers.

Around mid-morning I drove to Valerie Shoupe's. She answered the door in a bikini, partly covered up by a sarong that was draped over her shoulder. It was the sort of bikini parents refuse to buy for teenaged daughters. But she was a grown-up and anyway, she had the legs for it. She was drinking a Bloody Mary, and from the way she was standing, her hip and forearm resting against the door, I would have said maybe it wasn't her first.

"I've been going through Evan's things," she said as she showed me into the house, walking barefooted across the terrazzo floor. She led me onto the patio between the pool and Evan's guesthouse. We sat down among an arrangement of outdoor wicker furniture with over-stuffed white cushions.

"What happened?" She pointed to the gauze on the side of my head.

"A little run in with some of Junior's boys."

"Junior?"

"The one who's sent me that nasty note? The one who put a contract out on me?"

"My God, is it very-painful, Harry? You poor thing."

"It's not too bad."

"Have you seen a doctor?" The sympathy didn't come naturally to her.

"I'm fine."

She put a cigarette between her lips but had trouble lighting it. I think it was the flint this time. It was an expensive and unreliable gold lighter. I took it from her and managed to achieve ignition.

"So I don't suppose anything's come up with Bernie?" she asked.

"I'm working on it."

179

"I'm sorry, drink?"

"Whatever you're having," I replied.

She took a pitcher of Bloody Mary mix from a stainless steel fridge under an outdoor grill and poured it into a glass, then added vodka. She had a heavy hand with the vodka.

"Judging from all the dive equipment, I'd say Evan was mounting an expedition of some sort, that much seems pretty obvious," I said.

"I didn't know we were going to talk business."

"What else did you want to talk about?" I was trying to be polite.

"I don't know, things. I want to talk about you."

"There's nothing to talk about."

"I think there is."

I sighed. "Trust me, there isn't. How about we talk about your brother, so maybe if he is alive we have half a chance of finding him?"

"What did you want to know?"

"Think back again. Did he ever talk about what his plans were. Did he talk to you about Bernie Leach, or Clifford Mink, or Juri Epstein?"

"Really, I don't remember."

"It's important that you try. Things are starting to get a little dicey. If there's any chance you can tell me something I don't know, now would probably be a good time."

"You're sure you're okay?" She stroked the back of my head, then curled her index finger around my ear.

"Can't I tempt you with a swim, it's so hot."

"I don't really feel like going for a swim. Besides, I didn't bring a bathing suit."

"We don't need bathing suits."

"If we could just try to stay focused for a moment." I

180

looked at my watch.

"Going somewhere?"

"I have something later on."

"Harry McCoy, don't you find me the least bit attractive?"

"Very much so, but see, there's a professional element to our relationship." Now with a single tug the strap on her bikini top was released. She stood before me. "How about that swim?"

"Yes, how about it?" I said. I stood, picked her up in both arms, and heaved her into the pool.

"Harry!"

I picked up a towel and held it for her.

"You hired me to find your brother, and now I'm in it up to my neck, and you're not making my job any easier. In fact you're making it very difficult, if you know what I mean."

"No one's ever treated me like that," she said, climbing out of the pool.

"Maybe someone should have," I wrapped the towel around her. "I'm sorry, now about your brother?"

"The truth is I don't know anything about Evan's little side businesses, except he wanted to sell his stock in Salisbury Steel to fund them." She hesitated, drying her hair. "There is one thing, but I'm not sure it has to do with anything."

"What?"

"Wait here." She went into the house and I took a sip of my drink and looked out over the bay. When she returned she was holding a brown paper bag in her hands.

"What is it?"

She tossed it on the table.

It landed with a convincing thud. You didn't have to be

181

a metallurgist to know what it was. It was a gold ingot, 50 ounces and 99.99 percent pure, and there was no mint mark.

"Where'd you get this?"

"With his stuff. He had it hidden pretty good."

"How long have you had it?"

"A while."

"Why didn't you tell me?"

"I didn't know. Now, I still don't know, I didn't think it was anything. Now I wonder if one of Evan's hair brained schemes actually paid off."

"Who else knows about the gold?"

"I didn't tell anyone."

I stared into her eyes.

"I swear," she said.

"I need to go through your brother's papers, everything – his checkbook, files, diary," I said.

She frowned. "Now you're mad at me."

"I'm not mad at you. Did Evan keep a calendar, maybe?"

"Maybe." She trudged off like a child sent to bed and returned with a worn leather diplomat style case with two leather buckles. She undid the buckles and opened the case. There was an address book in it, but the address book was a bust. Just a few friends, and not many of those. Most of the listings were for local shops and tradesmen. Valerie started leafing through his checkbook. It was of the loose-leaf variety, three checks to a page. The check register went back nearly a year. Not knowing what she was looking for, she handed it to me.

Evan's checkbook had a balance of $16,000 and change. Then there were the usual payments to landscaping services, utilities and credit card bills. Once a week a check was written to cash, usually for 500 dollars.

She started stroking my head again. I had to hand it to her, she was persistent. I gently peeled her fingers off my head.

"You're no fun."

"I know. I need to see his rooms again. Maybe starting with his desk. Where did he usually do his paperwork?"

She led me across the patio through the French doors into the living room of the guesthouse. She gestured, drink in hand, to a fine curly maple desk. Georgian, if I knew anything about antique furniture, which I did, thanks to Fiona, the ex-girlfriend who had worked for an auction house in New York. It was a nice piece of furniture -- museum quality, probably.

I pulled out the chair and sat down, looking at the desk. There were a number of small drawers and cubbyholes, and larger drawers below and above them.

I looked at Valerie. "Do you mind?"

"Have at it."

I began with the top drawers, sifting through insurance bills, bank statements, checkbooks and the usual, and finally coming upon a plastic accordion file containing handwritten notes, newspaper clippings, and articles photocopied from books. It looked like research for the documentary film Evan had planned. I was searching in the right neighborhood.

Moving down to the cubbyholes, I found a photo of a ship and looked like it had been cut out of an old magazine. At the bottom of the photo was the name of the ship, the Josiah Long.

"What's the Josiah Long?" I asked.

She shrugged.

I pulled my smart phone out of my pocket and did a

Google search, It said the Josiah Long was a tramp steamer that was lost at sea in 1916, a day out of Havana, and was thought to have been torpedoed.

I checked the rest of the drawers, but found nothing. "This is it, all there is?"

She nodded her head. "Does it help," she said absently.

"I don't know," I said.

Valerie draped her arms around my neck. Confident of her considerable powers, she was doubling down.

"Valerie, this probably isn't such a good idea. You're a client. It could get complicated."

"Complicated?"

I cleared my throat and gently peeled her arms from my neck. Not an easy thing to do.

"Old desks like these usually have hidden drawers, have you checked them?"

"No, I mean, well, no."

"A desk like this has to have one," I said. "A space behind one of the drawers, or maybe a secret compartment that pops out, something like that."

"It never occurred to me to look," she answered, her finger resting on her lip. "I wouldn't put it past Dad not to tell me. I never could keep a secret."

While Valerie watched, I methodically probed with both hands into the recesses of the desk, looking for false backs or voids, but the drawers and pigeon holes went all the way to the back of the desk, ruling out that possibility. I looked at the joinery, searching for seams or joints that might suggest a hidden drawer.

I'd seen a similar desk where a concealed spring catch released a carved column to reveal a secret compartment. But I couldn't find anything like that on this desk. I tapped the center pilaster which divided the two doors to the

184

bookcase. It was hollow. Without me having to ask, Valerie dragged up a needlepoint footstool and I climbed up to examine the top of the desk. There were three brass spindles, one on each end and one in the middle of a pediment.

Grasping the center one I tried to turn it, with no luck. But when I tried to lift it, it did oblige me. The center pilaster slid forward, revealing a cedar box behind it. Gently I pulled it out and shook it.

There was something inside.

I handed it to Valerie and climbed off the stool. I let Valerie open it, gingerly pulling out a roll of brittle, yellowed papers delicately tied with a piece of red yarn. We unrolled them, carefully, on the desk.

The paper was heavy stationery, with an engraved logo, elaborate and old fashioned.

ST. CHARLES COKE WORKS
ROCHESTER, NEW YORK
AUGUST SALENBACH, PRESIDENT

"Coke?"

"Before the steel company. Coke's how they make coal, or something," she said. "Dad tried to explain it to me once."

I studied the paper. It looked like a purchase order for a large quantity of chemicals, like mercury sulphide and a bunch of other things.

"August Salenbach was your great-grandfather?"

"It's a name we don't use anymore."

"That's what the guy at your office told me."

"He wanted to sound more American. He changed it to Salisbury," she explained.

I rummaged through the other papers. They were in Spanish. They were dated 1916.

"They're receipts of some kind, commodities," I said.

"Commodities?" Valerie asked.

"Chemicals from the looks of it."

"That makes no sense."

"Anything else in there?" I asked.

Valerie held the box upside down and jiggled it. She grew more interested. There was something else, at the bottom, stuck. She reached a pencil in and fished it out. Whatever it was was wrapped in tissue. She carefully unwrapped it, unfolding the tissue paper and sliding the object gently into the palm of her hand.

It was a medal, black and white enamel with gold edging, the ribbon brittle with age. I couldn't read the writing on it, but I could recognize the medal's shape and Teutonic style.

"What is it?" she asked.

"Unless I'm mistaken, it's what they call a Knight's Cross."

"German?"

I nodded. "If I had to guess, maybe your great-grandfather's loyalties weren't exactly in the right place. Then again, the U.S. was neutral until 1917, maybe he was doing something diplomatic. No one ever said anything?"

"Nope." She put the medal on the desk. Like that, she had lost interest. She brushed up beside me, she still felt a little wet.

"Enough business. Are you sure I can't tempt you in that swim?"

"Well, it is pretty hot, maybe that wouldn't be such a terrible idea."

TWENTY-EIGHT

The wall of Lt. Commander Alex Rhinehart's office was decorated with framed photos of Coast Guard vessels and their crews standing at attention on the deck. As a Coast Guard officer, he'd been around: New York, Cape Cod, Bahrain, and now, Miami. My attention shifted to the window, and a beautiful view of the Intracoastal.

"Nice view," I said.

"Beats the family carpet business," said Rhinehart.

"Where would that be?"

"Paramus, New Jersey."

I nodded.

Rhinehart sat down in his swivel chair and rapped his knuckles on his desk. "The service has its advantages, but you never know when you might get socked with a twelve-month tour in the Aleutians. Okay, give it to me in a nutshell."

"We'd like to have a look aboard Rum Runner," I said.

"Yeah, Detective Esperanza told me. But she's not in charge, and the boat's a crime scene, I don't think they want people going aboard."

"Who's 'they'" I asked.

"You know, the brass at police headquarters. When they dropped it here they specifically said it was off limits. Besides, the cops have been through it already," Rhinehart said.

"They might have missed something," I replied.

Rhinehart leaned back in his chair and steepled his fingers. "Why the interest?"

"We think Evan Salisbury was doing salvage work. Four people are dead." I looked at Lopez. "Isn't that right?"

He counted them off with his fingers. "Andrew Bigelow, Demetri, Mink, and now Bernie Leach. Four."

"Four people. We think Russian gangsters are involved, but we don't know why. We're asking for help. We're interested in any charts, logs, or plot coordinates that might be programmed into the GPS," I said.

Rhinehart thought for a moment. "Russians, huh?"

"Maybe Juri Epstein, know him?"

Rhinehart chuckled. "Oh, yeah. Real smooth character, has a ginormous yacht in Miami Beach."

"We suspect another guy, Vladimir Drestikoff, everyone calls him Junior, is involved in a drug running operation with an outfit called Caribbean International."

"Interesting."

"So will you let us aboard?" I asked.

"Sure, I'm just busting your chops. Detective Esperanza said it was okay, but she said she'd appreciate it if you don't tell anyone how cooperative I am."

"Scout's honor," I said.

"You were a Boy Scout?"

"No, but I always admired their creed."

"That's good enough for me."

Rhinehart led us past a row of Coast Guard cutters to an area kept off limits by a chain link fence. We passed through the gate to where Rum Runner was tied up. Lopez and I climbed aboard and entered the cabin. The interior hadn't been cleaned since the shooting, the cushion on the bunk where Bigelow was killed was stained with dried blood. Rhinehart slid open a window to let in some air while I went to the 12 volt electrical panel mounted on the aft bulkhead. I flipped on the switch marked "NAV," then sat down at the navigation station, a small Formica covered desk to the right of the companionway. I took a deep breath and removed a notebook and pencil from my pocket.

Mounted above the desk were the usual instruments: a chrome clock and matching barometer, a meter that reported the hull speed and wind speed, a compass and a VHF radio. A GPS unit was installed beside it, and a spiral bound folio of charts was stowed above it. I took it out and quickly thumbed through the pages. I had the same book of charts aboard Hobo. It contained about 30 fold-out pages, enough to get you from Miami to the Dry Tortugas, and to all the Keys in between. I quickly flipped through the entire book, unfolding each chart as I went.

"What are you looking for?" asked Rhinehart.

"I don't even know."

The air in the cabin was still and stifling. Sweat was beginning to bead on my skin. I pressed the power button on the GPS and opened my notebook. Then I pushed a small button labeled "Memory." Normally, a series of numbers would display in sequence on the small LED screen, chart coordinates programmed into the device which allowed the captain to set a course. But no numbers appeared because the memory was empty.

"No luck, huh?" said Rhinehart.

I shook my head, then looked around the cabin, my eyes coming to rest on a bookshelf above the chart table. There were the usual volumes, books on seamanship and safety, a cookbook for yachtsmen, and some mysteries. There was a single chart, folded up and inserted in the row of books. I pulled it out and unfolded it. Penciled in on the margin were the initials J.L. and two sets of numbers, longitude and latitude.

189

Rhinehart looked over my shoulder. "J.L.? What the hell does that stand for?"

"In his papers, Salisbury had information on a ship called the Josiah Long."

Rhinehart made a dismissive wave. "That old scow's has been picked clean. People dive on her all the time. Don't think that's what you're looking for."

"Humor me," I said.

I spread the chart out on the table and found the coordinates. They were located on the other side of the Florida Straits on the Great Bahama Bank at a place called Devil's Reef. The reef was about 50 feet deep and was situated on a ridge that extended south, getting deeper and deeper, eventually dropping into the abyss of the deep ocean.

"Devil's Reef, sounds ominous," said Lopez.

I noticed a book on the shelf. It was titled *Shipwrecks - Florida and the Bahamas, 1900 - 1930.* I looked up Josiah Long, it said she disappeared between Miami and Havana in 1916. She was a tramp steamer, five thousand tons, and had operated mostly in the Caribbean. She'd been carrying iron ore when she went down, it said.

The patio of the Colonade Hotel on Ocean Drive attracted a mid-afternoon crowd of swimsuit models and other beautiful people. Consuela fit right in, except she was probably the only one carrying a 9mm pistol. It was hot, and she'd removed her jacket. She was wearing a tight fitting T-shirt and skirt, so I figured the weapon was in her bag. At least I hoped she was armed. I had a bad vibe. I was feeling paranoid about crowded public places.

"I spoke to a friend at the Bureau; he pulled some

records," she said.

"And?"

"Most of what he had was from World War Two, not World War One. Did you know the government had a file on Salenbach?"

I shook my head and flagged down a waitress. I ordered a beer, then turned back to Consuela.

"The file's been declassified. The government investigated him to make sure he wasn't a spy. Background checks, routine surveillance, a few interviews. Nothing bad came out, he was clean. His son, in fact, Evan senior, was in the army, served as an interpreter with the Third Army, even got decorated."

"They must have had some reason to suspect him in the first place. What about before that?"

"That's where I think we may have something," she said. "I did some digging. In 1914 and '15, he was part of a group that called itself the German American League, supported the old country, mostly financial assistance, humanitarian relief, sending supplies that people couldn't get in Germany, lobbying Congress and President Wilson to stay neutral."

"Think he was smuggling embargoed supplies?"

"Could be, or cash," said Consuela.

"Start in South America maybe, load up a freighter with raw materials and hope it got through. Anything else?" I asked.

"There's not much in the files. I don't know where that gets you."

"Any mention of a ship called the Josiah Long?" I asked.

"No, why?"

"Trying to put two and two together. It sank back in

1916. Salisbury was interested in it."

She shook her head. "I'll see what I can find out. Oh, and I guess there is something else. I'm officially off the case."

"Halloran?"

She nodded.

"Why would he do that?"

"Said he wants a new team on it. They're declaring Salisbury a fugitive. I've already turned over all my notes."

"Turned them over to whom?"

"Halloran."

"What does he have against you and Muldoon?"

"Said we weren't making enough progress, said we were on the wrong track. He's got us assigned to some routine homicide in the Latin Quarter. Some bullshit about allocating resources more effectively."

"What are you going to do?" I asked.

"What can I do? I don't think Salisbury had anything to do with Leach's murder, and now the trail'll get cold. I guess what I'm saying is if Salisbury is out there somewhere, still alive, it's up to you to find him."

"Any word on Junior's whereabouts?"

She shook her head. "He's dropped off the map. Probably thanks to you. It's like he never existed. Very strange. None of our informants knows anything. We went back to Caribbean International but no one had anything to say. No one knows anything about what happened."

"You believe them?"

"They're just working stiffs, Harry, packing crates and driving forklifts."

"So why would Arina go there?"

"She said she was looking for Junior, said he hasn't been around. I spoke to the manager, he checked out."

"Which leaves us nowhere."

Consuela took a sip of her iced tea and sat back in her chair. She closed her eyes and let the afternoon sun shine on her face.

"Harry," she said, her eyes still closed.

"Yes."

"I may be off the case, officially, but whatever you do, don't do it alone."

"Got any plans right now?" I asked.

"Thought I'd hang out with you."

So I took Consuela with me to see Claude Baptiste. We found him in the back of his shop wearing the same dirty blue lab coat and heavy rubber gloves. His skin was pale and sickly looking, like maybe the toxic chemicals were getting to him. He led us through the crowded back room to the table with the glass tank.

He reached into it and removed something.

"What is it?" I asked.

"Spoons. The item you brought in was a corroded mass of cutlery, must have been from a galley." He pointed to the glass tank. More spoons were suspended in the middle of the tank, between two plates of sheet iron. A wire connected the spoon to the 6-volt battery, another wire ran from the battery to the iron plates.

"There was some corrosion, but they didn't oxidize too badly. Nothing that a little good old nitric acid couldn't handle."

He handed me the spoon. It was in good condition, though it was still coated with a fine layer of corrosion.

"It should clean up under running water," he said, pointing to a metal sink.

I went to the sink and rubbed the spoon under the

water.

"Is it Spanish?" I asked.

"Oh no, you want to see an old Spanish spoon, look in the shop. The ones you have are newer."

He handed me a magnifying glass. It was simple in design, heavy, resembling the sort of institutional utensils you find in restaurants or schools. Rubbing the spoon with my thumb, the monogram "M" appeared.

"M," he said, "all of them."

"What does 'M' stand for?"

"I wondered that too, couldn't come up with an answer. Some kind of monogram, the name of a boat, or the company that owned it.

"Any ideas?"

Maybe the 'M' made me think of Uncle Mo. I thanked Claude and turned to Consuela. "I know who we can ask."

TWENTY-NINE

When it came to underwater archeology, Uncle Morris said he knew a guy named George Patterson, a professor at the university. Consuela and I drove south down Ponce de Leon Boulevard to the campus where we found Uncle Mo waiting for us in the parking lot of the building that housed the history department faculty.

Patterson was sitting at his desk when we walked in. He had disheveled white hair and a rumpled linen jacket. His lips were puckered around a cigar, and he was reading a book. He looked up as we entered.

"Hiya Mo."

"Hello yourself, how's the ancient world?"

"They're rioting in Greece."

"That's socialism for you," Mo said, and introduced us.

"Nancy's turning all politically correct on me at home, won't let me smoke my cigars in the house." He thought for a moment. "Well, I suppose I could if I wanted, but it's not worth the hassle." He used his hand to fan away the smoke. "Technically I shouldn't be smoking in here, either, university policy, or state law, not sure which, so don't say anything."

Patterson began clearing away papers and magazines so we could sit down. His desk was a mess, as were the bookshelves, books crammed wherever room could be found. There was a potted plant on the windowsill. It looked like it hadn't been watered in months.

"Excuse the mess," said Patterson, "getting ready for a trip. Me and the missus are going on a cruise."

"Where to?" asked Uncle Mo.

He ruffled through some papers and somehow found a brochure. It showed a beautiful ship with a red hull and clean white superstructure sailing in crystal blue waters. "The Ocean Star," he said.

He read aloud from the brochure. "'Explore the mysteries of ancient cities and civilizations as you travel in unsurpassed luxury through the azure blue waters of the Aegean' – I like that, azure blue waters - 'in the company of an expert staff of historians, naturalists and archaeologists accompanying you throughout the voyage, presenting lectures and answering your questions.' That's me, the expert staff," he stabbed the air with his cigar. "I'm just boning up for my lectures. All expenses paid in exchange for doing a series of three lectures. Not bad."

"We're here because we need some expert staff," said Uncle Mo.

"Shoot."

I handed him the spoon. "What do you make of this?"

"Looks like a spoon."

"Of course it's a spoon," said Uncle Mo. "We're interested in the monogram, 'M,'"

"Where'd you get it?"

"Evan Salisbury had it," said Uncle Mo.

The name drew a blank stare.

"You don't know who I mean?"

"Sure I know who he is. Same fella was behind that expedition to find the Natividad a few years back."

"Natividad?" I asked.

"Nuestra Senora de la Natividad. Folks have been searching for it for years. This Salisbury fellow interviewed me about it, said he wanted to make a documentary. This is a few years back."

He stood up and walked to a framed antique map of Florida on the wall. "The Spanish fleet of 1692 was driven against this stretch of coast around here," he used his cigar to point to an area along Key Largo.

"And Salisbury never found it?" I asked.

He shook his head. "There's probably a million wrecks in the ocean. Trying to find the one you want is next to impossible, and even if you do, chances are its unsalvageable, or not worth the cost. If it is, then you can be almost positive it's already been salvaged."

"Well, I don't think we're interested in the Nuestra de whatchamacallit," said Uncle Mo, "what about the Josiah Long?"

Patterson turned to me, "old tramp steamer."

"A what?" asked Consuela.

"Ocean freighter, "Patterson explained. "They call 'em tramps when they carry different cargoes depending on what people need."

He pulled an old ship recognition book out, again somehow finding it in a massive pile of books and papers. He leafed through the pages.

"310 feet, 3000 gross tons. Sailed between Liverpool and ports along the Central American isthmus. Built in 1899 for British owners, the Minerva Line." He looked up. "There's your 'M,' that was easy. Hang on."

Patterson turned to his computer and did a search. He found an online article and printed it out. It was called "Remembering the Tramp Steamer, a nostalgic look back at the early days of steel merchant ships." It was from the website of a publication called *The Journal of Maritime History*.

The author was Jerome Gurnee. The article featured

197

the author's collection of photographs and centered mostly on anecdotes about life at sea in an age gone by. There was a brief mention of the Josiah Long's sinking, that she disappeared in a storm off the Bahama Bank. The author was the grandson of the captain of the Josiah Long.

I read the small print at the bottom of the page. It said Jerome Gurnee was a retired merchant captain living in Naples, Florida.

Consuela looked at me. "What do you think?"

"I think I'm going to Naples."

THIRTY

I spent the night sipping whisky and leafing through Patterson's books on Florida's maritime history – they covered everything from Spanish galleons to the Bermuda triangle. Pretty dry reading, but I wanted a little background before going to Naples. I wondered why the hell Evan Salisbury was interested in this stuff? I could think of plenty of more interesting and rewarding activities that didn't require being submerged in cold water where sharks could bite you and you could get the bends or run out of air and drown. Tennis, for instance. Or collecting pottery. Maybe dog shows or wine tastings. But no, Evan Salisbury was different. Maybe his life was too comfortable, and safe, and he had to seek out danger and excitement to find meaning. But what danger had he found, I wondered? I dozed off sometime after midnight, a text on underwater salvage open and unread on my chest.

The morning sun cut through the starboard porthole to wake me up. I showered quickly and on my way to meet Lopez I stopped at a Starbuck's on Coral Way to pick up a coffee and some pastry. Ever the thoughtful employer. I found a parking space on a side street and hopped out. I bought the coffee and pastry, then headed back to the car. When I turned the corner I was standing face to face with Donny Peterson.

"If it isn't the doggie detective."

"Not a good time, Donny, I'm not looking for trouble today."

"We got unfinished business."

Coral Way, with its bustling shops, cafes and galleries, was just around the corner, but here, the side street was deserted.

"I'm not fighting with you Donny."

"Fine, we'll do it the civilized way, six rounds, Rubin's Gym."

"I'm not going six rounds with you."

"Four."

"No."

He looked disgusted. "That's what I figured. You're a pussy."

He put his head down and did what he did best: charged off-sides. For a split second, I felt like a quarterback about to get sacked. I rolled to my left and, to my amazement, Donny brushed past me and crashed head first into the side of the building. He collapsed on the ground.

I shook my head. "Donny, that's why you're never going to make the Hall of Fame," I thought. Then I called an ambulance.

The incident delayed our departure, but Lopez made up for it easily, driving like a maniac. We cruised west on I-75, mile after mile of Everglades, and arrived in Naples by noon, then found Gurnee's home, a Florida ranch house not far from downtown Naples, without any difficulty. A black woman in a pink nurse's uniform showed us to a back room with sliding glass windows that faced a canal. The room had a desk in it, and a computer, and bookshelves, and sitting in a recliner by the desk was Gurnee.

He was frail and had unruly white hair and a face deeply creased with wrinkles. He wore a button down shirt with a V-neck sweater and Bermuda shorts with cream colored rubber soled shoes that fastened with Velcro straps, and socks pulled up almost to his knees. I noticed a walker near his chair.

"Mr. Gurnee, you got visitors," said the nurse.

"Show them in, show them in," he said, pushing the lever on the recliner so he could get out of the chair. We shook hands.

"Harry McCoy," I said, "and this is my associate, Steve Lopez."

"Sit down, make yourself comfortable. Was the drive okay?"

We sat on the couch and I nodded. "Very good."

"I don't get many visitors these days. Don't get around much. Haven't been to Miami in years. But I keep busy. Guess how old I am."

I shook my head. "80?"

He looked at Lopez.

"78?"

"I'm 94-years old."

"You look very young for your age," Lopez said.

"Eh. I'm starting to feel it. Ida does the marketing, my link with the outside world is pretty much this." He tapped his computer. "So you say you read my article?"

"Yes, sir. As I said over the phone, we're looking for Evan Salisbury, and we think the Josiah Long may figure into our investigation."

I opened my file and handed him the papers and newspaper clipping. He shuffled slowly to his desk and sat down, studying them carefully while I looked out the window.

In the backyard, on a stand, was an old wooden ketch. It looked like she'd been there a while. She was dirty, her paint and varnish peeled by the sun. Gold letters on her stern spelled Rosy. I had a feeling Rosy might be Mrs. Gurnee but I didn't notice any Mrs. Gurnee around the house. I didn't ask. Mr. Gurnee must have noticed me looking at the boat.

"Getting too old for her. She's been out of the water too long. A boat needs to be in water, you know, least a wooden one does, or else the keel doesn't get supported, and she hogs. Terrible thing to see happen to a good boat. Terrible. "

He gestured to the walls. They were hung with paintings of ships. "When I retired I did a lot of painting, marine art, but I can't do it anymore. My hand shakes."

"When did you retire?"

"Almost 30 years ago. I was a captain, container ship, sailed around the world."

"And your grandfather was the captain of the Long?"

"That's right. I used to sail on a tramp, too, when I first started out, before the war. I was just a kid. When you get old you start to feel nostalgic. That's why I wrote the article. I'm always writing articles. Find out what I need to know on the computer."

He was interrupted when Ida, the nurse, entered.

"Mr. G, you take your pill?"

"Yeah, I took it."

"You sure?"

"Sure I'm sure."

She put her hand on her hip. "What time you take it?"

"Ten minutes ago."

She eyed him suspiciously. "Didn't you ask if they wanted something to drink?" She looked at Lopez and me. "Did he ask if you wanted something to drink? Can I get you something?"

202

Before I could answer Gurnee responded. "Bring us some coffee, and that bottle of Sambuca." He looked at his watch and nodded to himself. "It's late enough, I guess."

The nurse returned a few minutes later with a tray of coffee and a bottle of Sambuca. She poured the coffee, Gurnee carefully put in the Sambuca.

"So you're trying to figure out why someone named Evan Salisbury would be interested in the Josiah Long?" he asked.

I nodded.

"He's Salisbury Steel, right?"

"That's right."

"Big Florida family. Used to be the Salenbachs, they owned the Minerva Line, you know. They owned the Long, too."

"I hadn't known that," I replied. I wondered how Valerie could have not known that. I guess when you own enough stuff, you lose track.

"You said you thought Salisbury was exploring the Long?" he asked.

I nodded. "Why would he do that?" I asked.

Gurnee looked confused. "The Josiah Long's been explored umpteen times since she sank. There's nothing of value down there."

"Can you be sure?" asked Lopez.

"People do like to dive on her. See, she's deep, but not too deep, less than a hundred feet. She sank just on the edge of the shelf; a few miles to the west and she'd be in four hundred fathoms. Where she is she's shallow enough for divers to reach her but deep enough to still make it interesting. Mostly dive outfits out of the Bahamas, I guess. How do you know this Salisbury fellow was diving on the Josiah Long?"

203

"We found some spoons, silver spoons, with the monogram M. Minerva Shipping Lines, right?"

"Yeah, I guess." He thought for a moment.

"What is it?" I asked.

"Just thinking. There's a mystery surrounding the Long, you know. There was only one survivor from when she sank. It was during a storm, but there were rumors that she'd been torpedoed."

"So I understood."

"Divers didn't find her until 1960. Her hull's split open. From the damage, I always thought maybe she was torpedoed, or collided with something." An idea crossed his face. "You said M, huh?"

"That's right."

"It's probably nothing, but I've done a lot of research on naval vessels, and -"

He got up and walked over to his library. One entire wall of the room was floor to ceiling bookshelves. He scanned the books, then pulled one out, blowing dust from the top.

"If my memory serves me, M is the monogram for marine, or navy in German. In this case..." he flipped through the book "...the Kaiserliche Marine."

"What's that?" I asked.

Gurnee looked up from the book. "The Imperial German Navy."

I sat back in my chair as I tried to understand. "Why would Salisbury have a German spoon?"

"There were all sorts of U-boats operating in those waters. That's why some people, me included, have speculated the Josiah Long might have been torpedoed. See, she was an American ship, so if she was torpedoed, the Germans wouldn't have publicized it, not in 1916. If the U-

204

boat that sank her also sank - and lot of them did - then no one would ever have known what happened. I'm just thinking out loud, this is pure conjecture."

"If she was sunk by a U-boat, wouldn't you be able to tell from the damage?" I asked.

"Possibly, but maybe not after all this time," said Gurnee. "'Course, that doesn't settle the question of the spoons, unless…" He stopped speaking mid-sentence, deep in thought, then he continued. "There was a U-boat that went missing around that time. The U-168. It's something I'm kind of interested in."

Lopez leaned forward. "Now we're getting somewhere."

"Like I said, this is just speculation."

"How'd the U-168 sink?" he asked.

"She just disappeared," said Gurnee.

"So you think maybe Salisbury wasn't looking for the Long, but for the U-168?"

"Maybe. No German surface ships were sunk near the Long, so if this spoon is from the German navy, it could be a sub. The U-168 wasn't the kind of submarine you normally think of, she was a U-cruiser, also known as the Wilhelmshaven, converted from the Deutschland class of cargo subs. She carried cargo and was designed to get through the British blockade. She was famous, made two round trip to Mexico; nickel, tin, crude rubber, mercury."

Lopez sat back in his chair. "What kind of cargo would it have aboard that anyone would want after all these years? Mercury? What are you gonna do with that, make thermometers?"

I cleared my throat. "Gold." I said. "They'd want gold."

THIRTY-ONE

Lopez drove slower on the ride back to Miami. He was deep in thought, not fantasizing about winning the Daytona 500.

"I don't get it. If there was gold on this sub, and Salisbury found it, wouldn't it be in a vault, somewhere safe?"

"Maybe. Maybe he didn't find it yet."

"But you saw some of it."

"I don't know. Who knows where he got that. Apparently he was a gold bug."

"So why did he have all that shit about the Josiah Long?"

I stared out the window at the wire fence along the highway. "I don't know."

I got back to the marina late that afternoon. The place was deserted. I'd left that morning looking for answers, but had returned with more questions. I unlocked the gate, then heard someone coming in behind me. I was about to turn around when something hit me hard on the back of the head. The next thing I knew I was on the ground, trying to get up. Someone grabbed my windbreaker, ripping it, and punched me in the jaw. Again I tried to get up, slipped and fell again. I lifted my head. Then something hit me and everything went black.

I came to smelling smoke. Siegfried was standing on my chest, barking. I'd seen enough Lassie movies to know

206

what he was trying to tell me. Hobo was on fire.

Flames were coming from the galley. I stood up, the dizziness nearly overwhelming. I reached for the fire extinguisher, one I always kept in the cabin, but the plastic hook was empty, the fire extinguisher wasn't there. The flames were spreading fast, curling up onto the ceiling above me. The heat was scorching. It was time to get out. I picked up Siegfried and rushed clumsily up the companionway steps, then plunged feet first over the side. As I hit the water I heard the propane tank in the galley explode behind me.

The next thing I knew someone was holding smelling salts under my nose. He started asking questions I wasn't in the mood to answer.

"What's your name? Please tell us your name, sir."

I was on a chaise by the swimming pool, there were people standing over me. Someone told someone else to get a stretcher.

"How many fingers am I holding up?"

I brushed the digits away. There was a bitter taste in the corner of my mouth, a stinging sensation when I licked it.

A cop knelt beside the paramedic. I saw a blurry vision of Cameron behind him. Her clothes were wet, and so was her hair.

"Do you know your name?" asked the paramedic. He spoke to the man behind him. "He might have a concussion. Looks like third degree burns on his right leg, up near the crotch."

"My crotch?"

The paramedic looked up at Cameron, who had Siegfried in her arms. He was wrapped in a towel and shivering. "You the one who called?"

207

She nodded.

Another man spoke, louder and more determined.

"What's your name?" he began. "Sir, do you know your name?"

"Yes."

"Well, what is it?"

"Harry."

"Harry what?"

He was asking too much. Just Harry was enough, I decided.

"Harry, is that your boat?" someone else asked. He was a fireman in a yellow coat and helmet.

The medic was putting a bandage on my scalp. He was wearing rubber gloves with blood on the finger tips. I tried to get up, but my head felt like it had been strapped to the chair. I thought I was going to throw up.

Someone said something about a hospital. I struggled to my feet, trying to shake off the dizziness. The paramedic was surprised. He said it was adrenaline, and tried to ease me back to the chaise. I shook him off.

What was left of Hobo still burned. Firemen were trying to douse her with extinguishers, but it was too hot, they couldn't get close enough. A fire hose was being dragged across the pool deck, but Hobo was on her way down. With the sound of cracking wood, she dropped lower in the water, her timbers heaving and bending, and then the flames went out in a cloud of smoke as water from the bay seeped through the burned planking. Her charred hull settled on the muddy bottom, six feet down. The mast, sticking out of the water, canted grotesquely to one side.

THIRTY-TWO

I was sedated when I got to the hospital. I remember seeing Lopez, and Uncle Mo and Aunt Mimi, but I don't remember what we talked about. I spent a restless night, tossing and turning, wishing I had never heard of Junior, or Juri Epstein, or Pretzel Maker Peterson, and all the rest of them. I had had enough of bulletproof vests and death threats and everything in my life turning to shit. As far as I was concerned, Evan Salisbury was dead and there was nothing I could do to change that.

The next morning the doctor decided my burns weren't too bad and my vitals were fine. He gave me a jar of cream and after the nurse drove me crazy with my insurance information, they finally said I could go. I took off the flimsy hospital gown and tossed it in the corner of the room and changed into clothes Uncle Mo had brought. He and Aunt Mimi drove me home. Their home, because I didn't have a home anymore. I was officially homeless.

I walked slowly up the stairs to my new quarters. The bed had already been turned down. I collapsed, my sutured head resting heavily on the pillow. The room was all fancy chintz, English furniture and antique botanical prints. Uncle Morris brought more clothes for me to wear. Unfortunately we had the same shoe size, and he offered me an extra pair of white patent leather Gucci loafers, vintage, along with some of his shirts and trousers.

"Let's get you comfortable," said Aunt Mimi, returning with additional pillows and blankets which she adjusted all around me. Uncle Morris, trying to help, turned his attention to the air conditioner, which was set around 32 degrees Fahrenheit. Aunt Mimi adjusted the lights, trying every combination, and then she closed the drapes.

Uncle Morris tuned the TV to a fishing channel he liked. The fishermen were on a lake somewhere in northern Wisconsin. It was raining, and they were wearing camouflaged rain gear. Normally I would have liked it, but my head hurt. Uncle Morris gave me the remote control. I looked for the button marked "off" and pushed it.

"Now," Aunt Mimi said, sitting on the bed beside me and looking at me seriously, "is there anything else we can get you?"

"Maybe some blankets."

"Are you ready for more aspirin?"

"I think so."

"Water or juice?"

"Got any tequila in that bar of yours?"

"Doctor said not with the medication."

"Water, then."

"Aspirin and another blanket coming right up, and you said water, right?"

I closed my eyes feigning sleep until a few minutes later, sleep did overcome me.

I woke later that morning to Uncle Morris standing by my bed, the sun shining through the wooden shutters. Much of the pain and the nausea had worn off and I wasn't nearly as dizzy as before, though of course now I had a nasal drip from the room's frigid conditions. Aunt Mimi went to find some Robitussin. Each time I was settled in my bed, the pillows and covers just where I wanted them, she came in to see where she could make improvements. It was driving me crazy.

"Please," I said, "enough" I pulled on the blanket as she tried to tuck it in for the fourteenth time.

"He's not going to survive two days if you don't stop fussing over him," said Uncle Mo. Then he realized that the local news was on, he picked up the remote control and turned on the TV news. "Everyone be quiet!" he commanded to the otherwise silent room. We watched together. Eventually the newscaster got to me. There was a video of Hobo's charred remains; the reporter said it was a brutal attack and arson was suspected. Police were following leads, the usual stuff. I saw Lapidus on the dock, looking at Hobo. He had his pipe in his mouth. There was a cutaway of Virginia, sobbing. It was touching, really, while the reporter said something about "shocked neighbors" and ended hoping this was an isolated incident and not the work of a maniac on the loose. Then the camera cut to a shot of Lopez. He was looking at the charred remains of Hobo. I thought he looked dejected.

I took my first cautious steps out of bed. I pulled on a terry cloth bathrobe and crept across the cool tile floor to the back patio with a copy of the Herald. I established myself in a chair by the pool and delved into the Metro section. There was no mention of me or of Evan Salisbury. I put the paper down, draped my bathrobe over the chair and stepped into the pool. It stung a bit when water splashed on my head. I thought I'd been told that chlorine helped cuts heal, or was that saltwater? Either way the effect was invigorating. I didn't feel like doing my usual laps, the dead man's float was about all I could muster.

"You have visitors," said Aunt Mimi, standing by the pool.

Behind her was Consuela, her svelte figure silhouetted in the sun. She was standing next to Cameron.

"How do you feel?" Consuela asked.

"Just awesome."

"Please tell me it wasn't Donny?" asked Cameron.

I shook my head. "It doesn't seem like something he would do, and whoever did it left the dog. Plus I think he's on the disabled list, for a while anyway."

She didn't sound convinced. "He doesn't really care about the dog. Besides, if he took Siegfried, then we'd know it was him. If it was him then I brought this on you, I really am sorry."

"Police already questioned him," said Consuela. "He was home when it happened. Apparently he has an injured neck." She turned to me. "So who did attack you?"

"Someone trying to collect on that contract?"

Consuela shook her head. "Why would they set a fire, make it look like an accident?"

"You mean someone else wants me dead?"

"Please tell me the boat was insured," said Cameron.

"It was, but it won't be easy finding another boat like Hobo. Maybe I won't be leaving so soon after all. Did the police get any forensic evidence, not that I care?"

"There's not much left, Harry. They think he might have used something as simple as a bottle of lighter fluid on top of the stove. No prints, and no witnesses. Make it look like an accidental fire, that's probably why they didn't take your weapons, didn't want it to look like anybody was there. Whoever did it timed it perfectly, the marina was deserted."

A few minutes later Muldoon arrived. He was his usual cheery self.

"You're probably going to be feeling this for a long time. Recurring headaches, dizziness. Maybe for the rest of your life," he said. "I have a friend, had a concussion, never recovered a full sense of balance. But I guess you should consider yourself lucky, a concussion can lead to a hematoma, and kill you like that." He snapped his fingers. "Hell, even with the dog licking your face you might never have regained consciousness. You could have been incinerated, like a Viking funeral."

"Yeah, I feel lucky."

I climbed out of the pool and put on the terry cloth robe and a pair of dark glasses. Aunt Mimi brought a tray of Arnold Palmers and we sat down at the table by the pool.

"So you're still off the case?" I asked.

"Halloran's got two rookies on it, and it's low priority. You won't see much of them."

"Sounds like he's not too interested."

"Halloran's got political ambitions, and Juri Epstein is a mover and shaker. He has political muscle in this town. Halloran wants to steer things away from him, and any other Russians that might be involved. Makes the police look weak."

"Still no word on Junior?" I asked.

Muldoon shook his head. "Nada."

"So where does that leave us?"

"It doesn't leave us anywhere, where does it leave you?" he asked.

"I'm done. I intend to call Valerie Shoupe and advise her to find another private detective, though I think she would be well advised to save her money."

"You're quitting the case?" asked Muldoon.

"The case, Miami, everything. Isn't that what you advised me to do in the very beginning?"

"Yeah, but..." Muldoon started to speak.

"Lopez will be disappointed," said Consuela. "I think you two made a good team. He's pretty broken up over

213

this."

"He'll get over it."

"He said he was coming over later, said he still had a few leads to follow up on," said Consuela.

"Leads?"

"Said he wanted to do some surveillance at Earl's Boatyard, seeing as how that's where Mink met Salisbury in the first place."

Muldoon raised an eyebrow. "Earl Montgomery?"

"You know him?" she asked.

"Sure, used to be a cop before he went to his old man's boatyard."

"Miami PD?" I asked.

Muldoon nodded. "'Bout ten years ago. Got into trouble with Internal Affairs, never proved anything. But he was dirty. Word was he was involved in running grass up from Jamaica. Union wouldn't back him and eventually he had to resign."

Consuela's cell phone rang. She listened to the caller, then snapped the phone shut.

"Speak of the devil."

"Earl?"

She shook her head. "Junior."

"What about him?"

"He's not a missing person anymore."

"They found him?"

"Yeah, he's dead."

THIRTY-THREE

Murdered was more like it.

"We should check it out," said Muldoon, looking at me.

"What's all this 'we' shit?" I asked.

"Come with us, it would do you good," Consuela said.

"I thought you were off the case?"

"We are, doesn't mean we can't check it out. Come on."

Maybe she was right, I did feel like getting out of the house. Over the protestations of Aunt Mimi, I got dressed and we drove over to Point View, a small park just off Brickell. I knew the place, having jogged there a few times before I decided to give up jogging. It was a beautiful spot, a stretch of condos following a curving seawall facing Biscayne Bay, with expensive views of Virginia Key. From there you could see the old marine stadium, Fisher Island and beyond that, the Port of Miami, the cargo ship side, with its tall cranes and container ships outlined against the horizon. The sky had cleared, but a breeze persisted. A solitary gull worked his way south into the wind.

You usually found fishermen there, mostly from nearby Little Havana. It was a family spot. They came after work to fish, usually with hand lines, and have barbecues. They'd set up folding chairs, throw out their lines, and watch the sunset. I spotted the satellite dish of a news van telescoped in the air and found the crime scene not far from there. Consuela and Muldoon went to talk to the police already on the scene. I saw a brassy reporter I recognized from the local news who was filing her story, so I moseyed over and listened.

"This is Paula DeAngelo, reporting from a normally very peaceful stretch of coast off Biscayne Bay Drive, where police today recovered the body of a Miami man wanted for questioning about the recent disappearance of Miami business mogul Evan Salisbury. Residents who normally enjoy the scenic beauty and tranquility of this park were shocked by the news. Salisbury, as you may remember, disappeared last week, following a fatal shooting at a downtown marina. Sources inside police headquarters say the man found today matches the description of one Vladimir Drestikoff, also known as Junior, who had suspected links to crime organizations in New York before relocating to Miami last year. Though police stress he was not a suspect, he was wanted for questioning. We'll have more on this breaking story as the investigation continues. For now, this is Paula DeAngelo, reporting live from Biscayne Bay. Back to the studio. "

A young man, with a baseball cap turned sideways, ducked and weaved behind the newswoman, waving at the camera.

I walked up to him after the camera stopped recording. "What happened?"

"Floater," he said.

"Huh?"

"Dead guy, floating in the water. Fisherman spotted it, thought it was a lobster pot or something at first, then saw it was a dead guy, yo, freaked him out. He called the cops. Shark, or something, took some bites out of it, that's what he said, I ain't seen it. I don't wanna see that shit."

Yellow police tape had been strung between a row of palm trees to cordon off the crime scene. I found Muldoon walking back to the car.

"So I assume this wasn't an accidental drowning?" I asked.

"Well, let's see, two bullet holes in the back of his head, so, no."

"Execution?"

"I'd say."

"Strange timing, huh? I tell Epstein you're looking for Junior and... here's Junior."

"Like I said, Miami can be a very tough town."

I looked out over the bay. "Where do you think it happened?"

"Could have been miles from here. They'll check the currents, but they won't find the murder scene, if that's what you mean, unless someone talks, and no one talks."

"Maybe ballistics will match Andrew Bigelow."

"Yeah, and if you put a tooth under your pillow maybe the tooth fairy will come."

The next morning, after I smeared cream on my burns, I threw on a pair of Uncle Mo's Bermuda shorts, a golf shirt and a pair of brown loafers. I felt better knowing that Junior wasn't after me anymore, I wondered if that meant the contract on me was cancelled? I wasn't sure, it wasn't exactly what I'd studied in law school.

I decided I could do without the bulletproof vest. I'd been wearing it when I was pulled out of the water, and the hospital had given it to me in a plastic bag with my clothes. I decided to meet with Lopez later, return the vest, and tell him I was quitting the case.

I found the vest in the closet. Aunt Mimi had washed it to get the salt water out, and for once it didn't smell like dried sweat. Lopez's name was written on the inside of the vest and I remembered when we had stopped at his house, and he had given it to me. Then I sat down in the chair in my room holding it. Lopez was my partner. Was I letting him down? Like I had let Lucy down? I remembered what Consuela had said, that Lopez would be disappointed. She'd said he wanted to do surveillance at Earl's, alone, while I recuperated. Half an hour later, I had packed my car and was heading south on Route 1, dialing Lopez as I drove.

THIRTY-FOUR

I parked down a residential side street and removed from the backseat an aluminum folding chair, easel, and box of paints I had borrowed from Aunt Mimi. I walked to a small park overlooking the water. From the park I could see both Earl's dock and the front entrance to the boatyard about a hundred yards away. I set up a folding chair and an easel and my paints and put on a straw hat to complete the scene.

It wasn't a bad place to paint, there was an island in the distance, a dilapidated dock, a few sailboats at anchor, and some palm trees. I started on a watercolor of the waterfront with the palm trees in the foreground, sketching the scene lightly first, then mixing the paint. I worked slowly, so I wouldn't finish too soon, carefully observing every detail before making a brush stroke. It was the perfect cover.

I finished the first watercolor in about a half hour. No one had taken any interest in what I was doing, and no one had visited the park, it was too hot. I studied my work. It wasn't half bad. The colors in the water showed a nice touch, I thought, but the palm fronds could suggest a little more movement. I took out a second sheet of paper and made a pencil and watercolor study of the palm fronds, and after about a half hour of this I was satisfied, the palm fronds seemed to indicate the languid breeze, and the translucent green was just right.

I turned my attention to the reflection of the seawall on the still water, which was very dark in places. I experimented for a long time trying to get it right. I used two sheets of paper doing this, and almost forgot my main purpose, momentarily panicking that someone may have come and gone from the boatyard without me noticing. Then I started a second landscape. I was almost finished when a beat-up Buick pulled up in front of the boatyard. A large woman got out of the car. She had to bring both her feet out first, then heave herself up, holding onto the door frame. I recognized her as Earl's wife, Doreen.

She went into the boatyard and stayed until mid-morning. I was working on my fourth study when she hobbled out carrying a plastic cooler. I quickly bundled up my paints and easel, spilled the cup of water and hurried back to the car. A minute later I was tailing her southbound on Old Cutler Road. She pulled into the drive-through of a Burger King and bought an extra-large soda, then continued on.

After several miles she turned off on SW 184th Street in Cutler Ridge, and pulled into the driveway of a ranch house with a "for sale" sign planted in an overgrown and dried-out lawn. The "for sale" sign said "waterfront," and sure enough there was a canal behind the house, a ribbon of moisture cutting through the otherwise parched and lifeless landscape.

I pulled to a stop fifty yards past the driveway and observed as Doreen walked around the house toward the canal. Ahead, I noticed was an overpass crossing the same canal. There was a parking space there, which I took. I got out of the car and walked toward the overpass. When I got there, I crouched down behind the concrete guardrail. From here I could see the back of the house, a modest two or three-bedroom stucco with a pool half-filled with dirty water in the tiny backyard. There was a dock on the canal and a 30-foot cabin cruiser tied up. The cabin cruiser looked a lot newer and nicer than the house. It had oval shaped portholes in a large cabin in the bow, leaving room for a small aft deck. From the wheelhouse, curving stairs led into the forward cabin. There was a large swim platform on the stern.

There was a yellow wire running from the boat to an outlet on the dock so I figured the boat must be air-conditioned. No one could have stayed aboard otherwise, it would be like a fiberglass oven. The water in the canal was dark and still, though there must have been some current, because between the boat and the seawall discarded plastic bottles and rotten oranges had drifted.

Doreen stood on the dock and put her hand to her mouth like a megaphone. "You there or what!?"

A moment later Earl emerged from the cabin. He was wearing a Miami Heat sleeveless basketball shirt and plastic sandals, his hair was messed up and he was unshaven. He looked like he'd been sleeping. Doreen handed him the cooler and he held out his hand to help her aboard, which was dicey, given her substantial weight and shaky legs. They both descended into the cabin.

Less than five minutes later Doreen left. I stayed, but after about ten minutes I decided I couldn't remain in my vantage point for long. I was too exposed. Earl was on the boat for a reason, and Doreen had brought him a picnic basket -- perhaps he was planning on going somewhere. I went back to the car and consulted the map. The canal connected to the other canals winding through South Miami. There were a couple of ways to get into Biscayne Bay, but the most likely route was the Cutler Canal. Rather than stay where I was, I could stake out where the canal fed into the bay. I would need a boat.

An hour later Lopez met me at Uncle Mo's.

"Detective Esperanza said you were thinking of

quitting the case. Said you were feeling pretty low," he said.

"I was."

"So why the turn-around?"

I shrugged as I helped Lopez untie the canvas top to the boat. "I guess I never did thank you."

"For what?"

"Lending me your bulletproof vest."

"Like I said, I never wear it."

"Thanks anyway."

After we took off the cover from Uncle Mo's 22-foot Boston Whaler, which was on a boatlift, we lowered it into the water.

"You sure it's all tuned up and got gas?" asked Lopez.

"Pretty sure," I said.

I put a few fishing rods in the boat's fishing rod holders, for looks, and Aunt Mimi came rushing out with a bag of sandwiches and water. An hour later Lopez and I were anchored off the entrance to the canal, fishing. If anyone wondered, we were fishermen, goofing off on a weekday afternoon.

"Might as well use bait," said Lopez. "Seems stupid to have naked hooks in the water."

"I didn't have time for bait."

Lopez frowned. "Spot like this, catch a big red snapper. Don't you have a lure?"

"Aunt Mimi gave me some ham sandwiches," I said, "but we might get hungry later."

"Give me some of the ham."

I forfeited half a sandwich and watched Lopez put the sliced ham on the hook running the barb through it three or four times so maybe the ham wouldn't fall off. He put the hook in the water and waited a few minutes, then reeled it in to check the hook. The ham was gone.

"Something's down there," said Lopez.

I baited my own hook while Lopez put more ham on his hook.

"Never caught anything with ham before," I said.

Lopez was right, something was down there, kept nibbling at the bait, just enough to keep us interested, but after losing my bait for the third time I put the rod down and ate the rest of the ham sandwich.

We spent the next two hours pretending to fish, which isn't a lot of fun. Lopez kept reminding me to remember the tackle box next time. He said he was sure there were red snappers around, and told me about every fish he'd ever caught. As the afternoon wore on, I was about to throw in the towel.

"We got something," said Lopez.

"A fish?"

"Better."

He pointed toward shore. Earl's motorboat had appeared at the mouth of the canal. I started the engine and Lopez pulled up the anchor.

"Don't follow too close, set a different course, so he doesn't think we're following him," he said from the bow.

Dark clouds were blowing in from the west – afternoon rains on their way, but these looked more ominous that the usual passing showers. Earl exited the canal and headed south, so I set a southeasterly course. I didn't want to appear to be following him, but he was gradually getting farther away from us, and his boat was faster. He was headed along the coast, we were headed straight down the channel toward Elliott Key. After a few minutes I turned onto a parallel course and we were speeding across

Biscayne Bay. The water was smooth and still, and the wake sparkled in the sun, now low on the horizon. I had initially worried that Earl was simply headed to Earl's Boatyard, but I now saw he was headed nowhere near it.

"Think he's back in the drug running game?" asked Lopez. He had to shout to be heard over the engine and the rushing wind.

"I guess we'll soon find out."

"He heads out to sea you can't follow, not in this," he said.

"We'll do the best we can."

Lopez pressed his back against the center console and drew his pistol. He checked to make sure there was a bullet in the chamber, then slipped the gun into its holster, which was clipped to his belt.

"He's running drugs, I should have brought the AR-15," he said.

"You have an AR-15?"

"At home."

"Not going to do us any good there."

"What?"

"Not going to do us any good there!" I repeated.

He shook his head. "Hope he doesn't have an Uzi, is all."

As I steered, Lopez followed Earl's boat with a pair of binoculars. He was headed toward a sparsely populated stretch of coast.

I removed a chart from the console and folded it so I could look at it without it blowing away. Below Key Biscayne there were few channels connecting Biscayne Bay to the open ocean. A small boat could cross the shoals, but not a large one. Further south was Featherbed Shoals, with a single narrow channel that led south toward Key Largo. I wondered where he was going.

Lopez peered through the binoculars, watching him. After a few minutes, he said, "he's slowing down."

I took the binoculars from Lopez. In the dimming light, I saw the wake behind Earl's boat die down, the boat had dropped lower in the water and slowed. He motored up to a small, flat-roofed shack. It was supported about twelve feet above the water by pilings. There was a dock below it and wooden stairs leading up to a deck. Earl tied up at the dock. A hundred yards away, on the shore, stood what might have been an old fish factory, a dilapidated building made of rusted, weather-beaten corrugated tin.

"What the hell's he doing?"

Lopez shrugged. "Maybe it's a rendezvous, let's stick around, see who shows."

I pulled back on the throttle. There was a small inlet among the mangroves along the shore. I motored into it, killed the engine and Lopez threw out the anchor, which gripped right away on the sandy bottom.

We watched for about half an hour, then the rain started. A few large drops at first, then there was a ripping sound in the clouds and the rain came down like a curtain.

Lopez wiped the rain from his face. "We not gonna see shit in this, let's move closer."

He pulled up the anchor and we motored slowly through the rain toward the house on stilts. When we were very close I turned toward shore and killed the engine and we drifted once again into the mangroves. From there we watched the stilt house. A few minutes later Earl came down the stairs. He uncleated the lines to his boat and climbed aboard, then he started the engine and motored away, quickly disappearing.

"So much for a rendezvous," said Lopez.

"What the hell is he doing?" I asked.

"Let's find out."

We waited a couple of minutes, then I turned the ignition. We motored slowly to the house, the rain was coming down hard now, pelting the deck of the boat and the dock as I tied up. My pistol in hand, I climbed the stairs to the deck. An unlocked door led into the house, revealing a large room with shuttered screen windows on three sides. The place had once been some kind of social club. There was a disco ball hanging from the rafters, and a bar along one wall, but now it was abandoned, and smelled like dried fish guts. A door led to another room. It was closed and locked. I heaved my shoulder against it and the old dried-out wood around the lock gave easily.

Facing me, blindfolded, was Evan Salisbury.

He was bound and gagged and had a few days growth of beard. There was a chain padlocked around his ankle. At the other end of the chain was a 100-pound mushroom anchor. I pulled the blindfold off and removed the gag. He looked more astonished than I was.

"Harry!"

I talked fast. "Your sister hired me to find you. Let's get out of here."

He breathed a sigh of relief. "I thought you were them."

"You mean Earl? He left."

"Whoever it was, he's coming back."

I was sizing up the chain. "When?"

"Soon. He came to check on me, then get the rest of them. I think there's a main house on shore. They come back and forth. They've been trying to starve me, get me to talk. I've been holding out, otherwise I thought they'd kill me. Did you bring water?"

226

There wasn't time for him to explain things.

"We'll get you all the water you want as soon as we get out of here. How much time do you think we have?"

"Not a lot."

I tried to loosen the shackle that linked the chain to the anchor. There was no way it was coming loose. It had been bent with a hammer.

"They left me alone sometimes. That's why the anchor," Evan said.

Even if I could have taken the anchor off, the chain would have been heavy enough to pull Evan under, just not as fast. I examined the padlock.

"Stand back," said Lopez, one step ahead of me, "I'll shoot the motherfucker."

"It's hardened steel," said Salisbury.

He aimed his automatic at the shackle and fired six well-aimed shots. The bullets didn't make a scratch, but went straight through the plywood floor.

"Time to go," I said. "We'll carry it."

I picked up the mushroom anchor and as much chain as I could handle. Lopez picked up the rest of it. Together Salisbury and I descended the stairs, now slick with rain. I had the anchor in my arms, and couldn't hold the rail. The weight of the anchor made it hard to walk on the slippery wood. I took my first step and my foot shot out from under me. I slid down the steps toward the dock, still clutching the anchor as I thumped over the wooden stairs. The anchor slipped from my arms and I watched, horrified, as it skidded across the dock and plunged over the side. Lopez grabbed the chain and managed to stop it, his foot jammed against the railing. We pulled the anchor back onto the dock.

We hurried across the wet floating dock, which tipped

227

steeply under the weight of three men and the anchor, Salisbury holding his chain like a convict. Lopez helped him into the boat, then jumped in after him. I handed the anchor to Lopez and was the last in. In the invisible distance, I heard an approaching motorboat. Had they heard the shots? I wondered. Sound travels strangely on the water, but it was still raining hard, maybe they hadn't. It didn't matter, the boat was getting closer.

"Let's move," said Lopez.

I turned the key.

Nothing.

Lopez froze, locking eyes with me for a moment, then he drew his automatic and checked the safety.

We had just moments to choose our ground. I looked around. There were a few weathered planks spanning the pilings at the end of the house where we might hide, especially in the dim light. Lopez saw it too and helped me push the boat into position.

Through the spaces in the boards we watched as the boat approached, The engine idled and three men jumped onto the dock. One of them was Earl. The other two I didn't recognize, but they were all armed.

"Hey dipshits, don't forget to put your hood on," one of them said.

"It's too fucking hot."

"Just do it, asshole."

Earl and one of the other men slipped on knitted ski masks.

When the men climbed the stairs, I pushed off from behind the wall and drifted into the darkness, paddling with an oar I had found in the bottom of the boat. The current was strong, and soon we were well away from the house. I tried the engine again, and this time, thank God, it started, or we would have been floating in Biscayne Bay for hours. I pushed the throttle and sped away as fast as the boat would take us.

THIRTY-FIVE

"Why'd you run?" It was the question on everyone's mind. I asked it.

Evan looked confused. We were in the living room. Salisbury was showered and dressed like me, courtesy of the "Morris Marsh Thrift Shop." I'd decided to wait until Consuela and Muldoon arrived for the official questioning. I wanted it on the record so Evan would be cleared in Leach's murder investigation.

"We assumed you knew they murdered Bigelow the night you disappeared," said Consuela.

He shook his head. "No."

"So why weren't you on the boat when they came?"

"I never sleep on the boat, only Andy did."

"Why go to the model home in Coral Gables, why not go to your sister's?" I asked.

"I'd gotten some threatening phone calls, that's why I moved the boat. I didn't want anyone following me, either. I've used that house before. Anyway, I woke up the next morning, some men came to the house, they shot me with one of those electric guns, and the next things I knew I was chained up where you found me."

Muldoon was taking notes. "Can you give us a description of the men who kidnapped you?"

"No. They were wearing stockings over their heads, which scared the shit out of me. I never did see what any of them looked like."

Muldoon looked up at me. "Probably the same guys who tried to kill you."

"Did any of them have a Russian accent?" I asked.

"No."

"The man who led us to you is Earl Montgomery, you know him?" I asked.

Salisbury nodded. "Sure, who doesn't?"

"We've put out an arrest warrant," said Consuela, "but it looks like he's pulled a disappearing act. Probably a wise move."

"So they killed Bernie?" asked Evan.

I nodded. "With your gun."

Uncle Morris, all action when we arrived, was now dozing in an armchair. His head was cocked back, his mouth open, and he was snoring. He woke with a start to the sound of ice cubes being dropped into a martini shaker. Official meetings like this are so much better when drinks are served. Anyway, it was a celebration of sorts. Evan Salisbury was alive. Saved by Lopez and me, and we would be $50,000 richer because of it. I'd already made the call to Valerie Shoupe.

Evan took a sip of his drink. "This whole thing is nuts."

Muldoon looked up from his notepad. "You said you were threatened. By whom? About what?"

"I don't know. They said they knew what I was doing, and if I didn't do as they said or if I went to the police they'd kill me and my whole family."

"And so you didn't go to the police?"

He shook his head.

"That was stupid," said Muldoon.

"Of course."

"Why kidnap you?" Muldoon asked. I already had it pretty well figured out, so I was letting Consuela and Muldoon ask most of the questions.

231

"Obviously they caught wind of my activities. I had a couple of guys working on the boat, someone must have blabbed. Maybe Andy talked to that guy Clifford Mink, I always had a bad feeling about that guy. Anyway, I told them I didn't know where the sub was. They didn't believe me, said they'd be back. They wouldn't let me eat. They said eventually I'd tell them everything I knew. They were right, I would have if I had known."

"What did they want to know?"

He took a sip of his drink. "Where the gold is."

There was quiet in the room. Gold will do that. Muldoon and Consuela exchanged glances. Then Consuela looked at me. I shot a glance at Lopez, just to keep it going.

"Can this part be off the record?" asked Evan.

"Anything you say is on the record," said Muldoon.

"Oh hell, I don't care anymore. I was interested in salvaging a shipment of gold."

"From the U-168?" I asked.

Evan choked on the vodka. "How'd you know that?"

"While you've been tied up, Lopez and I have been investigating."

"I'm impressed. Problem is, I don't know exactly where it is."

"But your sister showed me a gold bar."

Evan shook his head. "That was my grandfather's. I didn't get that from the sub."

"But you dove on the sub, we found the silver spoons you recovered."

He nodded. "Now I'm really impressed. Yes, I've been to the sub, but only once. We didn't have time to fully excavate it, but I'm pretty sure the gold is still there. No one else knows where the sub is."

"Except you?" asked Lopez.

"I don't, in fact. Well, I have a pretty good idea where it is. Bernie was the navigator, he kept the coordinates in his head, said it was safer that way. Now, we'll have to find it all over again."

I guess I looked confused. Evan explained.

"Grandfather Salenbach traded with the Germans, sold them raw materials they couldn't get because of the blockade. The cargo would be off-loaded at sea. The Germans always paid in gold."

I finished the story for him. "But the last time, the Josiah Long sank before the cargo could be off-loaded."

"You got it. Best I can tell, the ship and the submarine collided attempting to find each other. My grandfather knew from the lone survivor. He paid him off and kept it a secret. He never could recover the gold. But there was a file."

"And you found out about it from your father's papers and thought you'd locate it?"

"That was the general idea."

THIRTY-SIX

That evening I developed a plan. We needed a professional diver, and Lopez said he knew a guy. He had a friend who ran a dive shop in Coconut Grove. Consuela had the day off and agreed to join us. Muldoon took a pass, said he had a date with a TV, a couch, and a football game, but Evan agreed to join us. The next morning, bright and early, I picked Consuela up at her house.

"You don't have to do this, you know, the job is over," said Consuela as we drove to the dive shop.

"I want to take it all the way."

"With Junior dead, you probably don't have to worry anymore."

"I want to catch whoever killed Andrew Bigelow, and kidnapped Evan Salisbury. I want closure."

"You want the gold."

"I want the gold."

The dive shop was located in a giant Quonset hut partitioned into a number of small commercial spaces located near the marina in Coconut Grove. The other tenants were mostly sailmakers, boat brokers, and mechanics. Sinclair Ocean Expedition occupied one large room. There was an old desk, a rattan couch that might have been salvaged from a dumpster somewhere, and two decomposing wicker chairs. On the walls were faded underwater photographs. A sign above the couch read "Sinclair Ocean Expeditions." The word "expedition" sounded a little grandiose, I thought.

Two men in bathing suits and flip-flops were sitting on the sofa. One with a grizzled beard and dark tan was engrossed in the morning paper. He looked like a country western singer. The other was leafing through a dog-eared Victoria's Secret catalog. He was more interested in the catalog than anything else. Eventually the man with his nose in the paper looked up and smiled.

"Charlie Sinclair?" I asked.

"You're lookin' at him."

"I'm Harry McCoy, I called earlier." I introduced Evan and Consuela.

Thirty minutes later we were aboard the dive boat called *Pathfinder*, motoring out of the channel below the high rise buildings that lined the shore of Coconut Grove. Sinclair inched the throttle forward and the boat began to plane over the waves through Biscayne Channel, past the cluster of platform houses called Stiltsville. They'd been built mostly during prohibition for wild parties. Gradually, over the years, they'd been thinned out by storms, but a few were still standing. It was just a matter of time until the last one was swallowed by the sea.

I stood by the skipper and watched the glass skyscrapers of downtown Coconut Grove getting smaller and smaller. I liked the boat. Pathfinder was state of the art. She was large enough and well enough equipped to stay out for a week or more.

"Fast boat," I said.

"Name of the game," replied Charlie. "Get out there fast and people can spend more time in the water. I usually try to do two trips a day, one in the morning, one after lunch."

It was time to suit up. Consuela slipped off her cotton beach shirt, revealing a red bikini and a leather shoulder

235

holster. It was a great look.

"Mystery solved. So you wear a shoulder holster under your shirt?" I asked.

Her mouth curled in a smile. "You don't know much about women's fashion, do you?"

"I know a little about leather straps, and those must chafe."

"They're lined," she said.

I looked closer. Sure enough, it was a satin-lined custom-made mesh shoulder holster, which explained how she could conceal her 9 mm and still show off her figure. She handed the pistol to Evan and asked him not to shoot anyone by accident.

Fifteen minutes later, we arrived at the first location. An idyllic spot, the lush palm trees of Key Biscayne in the background. The water was calm and clear and reflected the strong rays of the sun. Kevin hooked up to the boat's pre-positioned mooring tackle and Charlie donned his tank and stepped into the water. He disappeared for a few minutes, then his head popped up and he gave the okay sign. The charter group entered the water like so many penguins.

In the water, I could see about 20 feet. Beyond that, figures disappeared into a thickening haze. In pairs, the divers slowly made their descents, following the guide-line that was tethered between the bottom and a small buoy. Then an old tug came into view, a small school of tarpon hovering above it watching us as I held Consuela's hand and we floated, weightless, together. I let go of her hand and rolled upside down, and saw her silhouetted against the surface. She kicked her fins and rolled beneath me, then blew bubbles and descended deeper, her finger beckoning me to follow. How could I resist? It was like a commercial for Club Med.

Sinclair must have dived the tug a hundred times, but went through the motions of exploring it for the first time, leading us first through the wheel house, then all around the deck pointing out a moray eel, some little orange fishes, and sea horses. We saw Sinclair and followed him. He had an ease of movement underwater, like a sea lion, I imagined, hopeless on the beach but graceful below the waves.

When our air was almost gone we ascended to the boat where we basked quietly in the sun. Then Charlie pulled up the anchor and we headed west toward Coconut Grove.

I turned to Evan. "What do you think?"

"It's perfect."

The next day we had all our gear stowed aboard Pathfinder while it was still dark. Amazing how ten grand in cash can make a tight schedule loosen up. The sky was clear and the sea calm as the boat slipped her lines and left the harbor.

Over coffee in the cabin Evan and I went over the plan. The crew crowded around the table. There were six of us. A good crew, and we'd kept it as small as possible: Evan, who still hadn't recovered from his ordeal, was essential. Lopez, despite his misgivings, had agreed to come along. He wasn't a diver, but could handle trouble if it came our way. Consuela, my idea. Charlie, because it was his boat. And Kevin, Charlie's pimply deck hand, who knew how to work the computer.

Charlie had taped a diagram of U-168 on the bulkhead so everyone could see it. Kevin studied it closely and whistled.

"How much you think she's worth?"

237

"Back in 1916, about three million," said Evan.

"How much now?" asked Consuela.

"Figure maybe a hundred million."

That brought a whistle from Charlie. He was a better whistler than Kevin.

"Tell us more about the sub," said Consuela, heating coffee in the galley.

"What do you want to know?" Evan asked.

"How do we get in, for starters?" asked Charlie.

Evan pointed to the diagram. "The hatches are located here, here, and here, but the hull is broken open and we can swim right in."

"Aren't there rules about this?" asked Consuela. "I mean aren't these Bahamian waters?"

"The Bahamians think they are, the US government has another point of view," said Charlie, "but it's beside the point. Germany would never grant salvage rights on a sunken warship. It's a military grave."

Lopez was leaning against the bulkhead, listening. "So we find this gold we get to keep it?"

"The idea behind salvage law is you want there to be an incentive for people to rescue ships in storms and recover cargo. To do that you offer compensation," I explained.

"How much?" asked Lopez.

"It varies. Usually whoever mounts the recovery works out an agreement beforehand," said Evan.

"But we don't have an agreement," said Lopez.

"No, we don't," replied Evan.

"So we can't keep the gold if we find it?" asked Kevin.

"We'll have to see. One would think the German government will be grateful if we do end up finding it, I'd say we end up with a pretty good chunk," I replied.

238

Charlie cleared his throat. "We still gotta find the gold before someone decides how much we get to keep. I know Devil's Reef pretty well, but I never seen no sub there. Water gets pretty deep, too. Kevin, what about weather?"

"Storm's heading our way, maybe 36 hours," he reported.

"That's not a lot of time, so how exactly do we locate the wreck?" asked Consuela.

"Sidecar sonar," said Evan, nodding toward the four-foot torpedo shaped object lying on the floor of the cabin. "The sonar will feed back to Kevin's laptop, he'll monitor it in the wheelhouse."

"Any more questions?" I asked. No one spoke up, so I decided to end the meeting. "We won't be there for a few hours, I suggest everybody get some rest."

I took my own advice. The sun was just coming up and I was bushed. I found the last empty bunk amid the life jackets in the forward cabin and climbed in. It was damp, and smelled of seawater. But it was warm, and soft, and reassuringly familiar. Consuela climbed in after me. She was warm and soft too. Within minutes, we were both sound asleep.

I woke to the realization that the boat had slowed. Consuela was gone, and Pathfinder was rocking over long, gentle swells. I climbed out of the bunk and yawned, scratching my head, then climbed up to the wheelhouse. We were in a fog bank, the sea around us was dark and smooth. The air felt cool and damp against my face.

Kevin and Charlie were on the aft deck, rigging the sled that housed Evan's sonar device. I watched as they secured it to a cable and then helped them lift it over the stern. Carefully, they played out the cable. The sled disappeared from view as the cable unrolled off its drum. When they

239

had let out a hundred feet, they stopped.

Kevin looked out at the fog bank.

"What is it?" I asked.

"Nothing, thought I heard something. Kind of creepy out here in the fog."

I watched as Kevin plugged wires into the back of his laptop, which he had set up by the wheel. I watched the screen for a while, ghostly white blurs with black shadows. Then I got bored doing that so I went below to the main cabin and sat down at the chart table. The GPS was turned on, displaying our current position and heading. I plotted it on the chart. We had crossed the straits in good time, and were right on the edge of the Bahama Banks. Here the ocean floor rose dramatically. The depth gauge read 1550 feet. Soon, when we hit the shelf, that number would change to more like a hundred feet, then even less.

I pulled on a sweatshirt. Lopez was in his bunk, his eyes closed, his skin green. He looked miserable.

"Dramamine hasn't kicked in yet, huh?

He moaned.

"Don't worry, you'll get your sea legs."

I'd seen stronger men than he incapacitated by seasickness. The slow motion of the boat rocking back and forth didn't help. Or maybe it was the diesel fumes.

He turned over and covered his head with a life jacket.

I returned topside and joined the others back in the wheelhouse. The boat had reduced speed further when the sled was lowered, and the rocking motion had intensified. Charlie watched the GPS coordinates on the instrument panel as he steered the wheel.

"You might be seeing something soon," he said.

We trolled along slowly as Kevin watched the sonar screen, frequently adjusting the tuning, and we were quiet.

Twenty minutes later, he broke the silence.

"Something's down there," he said, "We're right on top of it."

I looked at the depth gauge: 95 feet. All at once everything was activity. Charlie circled the boat around and stopped. Kevin dropped the heaviest anchor we had over the bow, then stood by as the line paid out. Charlie began stuffing himself into a wet suit. I helped him with his fins and tank. He lowered his mask and unceremoniously dropped backwards into the water.

"Aren't you always supposed to dive with a buddy?" Consuela asked.

"Technically," replied Kevin.

Then we waited, watching the surface of the water for bubbles. Fifteen minutes later Charlie's hooded head popped up just off the stern. He swam toward the stern of the boat and heaved himself onto the dive platform. He waited until he was out of his tank and vest, and had pulled off his hood before speaking. There were red marks where the water pressure had pushed the rubber mask into his face.

"It's the Josiah Long, no doubt in my mind. Just like the picture. Superstructure's intact, the right length, it's her all right. Big gaping hole in her bow, resting on a coral reef, right where she was supposed to be.

"How was the visibility?" I asked.

Charlie wiggled his hand. "Not so good, 20 feet maybe, tops."

He stripped out of the wet suit and took the wheel. I helped Consuela with the anchor, turning the line around the automatic windless and hauling away as Charlie brought the engine back to life. Five minutes later, out of breath and the anchor stowed, I joined Evan and Kevin at

241

the nav station.

"So that's point A," said Evan, "which means U-168 is in this general vicinity." He pointed to an area south of our present position. "This is where we look."

We spent the afternoon taking turns on the aft deck monitoring the sonar cable. When it wasn't my turn to watch the cable I sat in the cabin reading my diver's guide as the boat rolled over large gentle swells. The monotony of life at sea. Occasionally someone turned on the VHF radio and tuned in to the weather report. It sounded like a robot speaking. It was the same all day and it was starting to make me more than a little nervous.

"The following is an advisory for all vessels operating between Jupiter Inlet and Cape Sable, including Florida Bay. A small craft advisory is in effect for Friday and Saturday, expect winds to reach 20 to 30 knots, with gusts of 45 to 50, and seas of 8 to 10 feet. A tropical storm warning is in effect...."

I turned it off, and went to help Consuela in the galley. I came up behind her and put my arms around her. She bent her head down to rest on my shoulder.

"Can I help?"

"You can chop this onion."

"How's Lopez?"

"He said he doesn't want dinner."

"I'll bring him some bread and water."

"And aspirin."

"And Evan?'

"Happy as a clam, watching the radar thingy."

She turned and faced me, and kissed me on the lips. "I'm glad I came," she said, "now go on, I need to cook."

After dinner of penne and sausages we shifted to a two-

242

hour watch, and everyone else except Charlie and me went to bed. We followed our pre-determined course, and watched the computer screen for any blip. There was no wind, so the surface of the sea was smooth, though it heaved gently. The stillness of the air portended weather to come.

"Gets bad, we head for the Bahamas," said Charlie.

I nodded.

That was about it. Charlie was not much of a conversationalist. So we sat looking at the laptop and checking the cable, foregoing the necessity of small talk. Except after about an hour Charlie said, "Knew a girl once in the Bahamas."

"Did you?"

He nodded. "She was quite a woman."

"What was her name?"

"Isabel."

"What happened?"

"She drifted away. That was years ago. Years and years ago."

Then he drifted away too, with his memories, and I didn't say anything. Around midnight Consuela came up. Her hair was rumpled and she looked groggy.

"Why aren't you sleeping? You've got a couple of hours yet," I said.

"Don't want to miss anything. How about some coffee?"

"Sounds great," Charlie said, rubbing his eyes.

"Me too."

She came back a few minutes later with three mugs of coffee. I warmed my hands against the heavy porcelain.

"Anything yet?" she asked. Her face was bathed in the dull green light from the computer monitor.

Charlie shook his head. "This may take a while. It's never easy to find something."

"But wouldn't they have sunk pretty close together where they collided?" asked Consuela.

"They might have, but they didn't. One of them, maybe both, managed to stay afloat for a while, drifting as they sank. Who knows."

We were on our second cup of coffee when dawn started to break with gray clouds overhead and the wind picking up. The morning wore on without any contact from the sonar, the weather gradually worsening, the clouds in the distance getting darker. We ate black beans and rice for lunch at noon. Afterwards, I was sitting in the wheelhouse wondering why we couldn't have stowed cold beer on board, when I noticed Kevin begin to fine-tune the adjustments on the laptops controls. I watched him without saying anything. The expression on his face turned serious. He suddenly sat up.

"Charlie," he said quietly.

"Yo."

"I'm getting something, almost as strong as the last one."

"How deep?" asked Charlie.

"One-ten."

They huddled over the laptop and there was much discussion. It was decided that the squiggly lines that looked like a broken TV were really something like a U-boat. I went to the chart table and noted our position on the chart. When I returned topside, everyone was on deck. Even Lopez, who helped Evan and Kevin haul in and secure the sonar to the side of the boat. Lopez paused at the rail, closing his eyes and breathing deeply.

Evan went to the bow, ready to let go the anchor as

Charlie circled. At a shout from Charlie he heaved it over the side. All we would have to do is follow the anchor line to the bottom. Charlie cut the engine and waited as Evan set the anchor. Then Charlie picked up his wetsuit and started putting it on.

"We don't have a lot of time, so I'm gonna have a quick look-see," he said as I helped him zip it up.

The fog seemed thicker here than at the previous site. It was cold, and a wind was now stirring up a heavy chop.

"Shouldn't someone go with you?"

"Let's conserve our divers for the salvage. This is just a quick peek."

I knew it was wrong, but Charlie was the captain, and sure of himself. Hard to argue.

"Stay on the rope at all costs, I don't want you drifting away from the boat in this stuff," I said, "we might never find you."

With a quick thumbs up he disappeared below the surface.

THIRTY-SEVEN

This time, the dive was deeper, and would take longer to reach the bottom. And Charlie would have to take his time ascending. Consuela and I pulled on our own wet suits while we waited.

Ten minutes passed.

Twenty.

Twenty-five.

Finally Charlie's head popped back up. I reached down and grabbed him by the top of his tank and Evan and I pulled him aboard. He struggled to hold his balance with the heavy tank strapped to his back as he caught his breath.

"She's broken open, just like you said," he sputtered.

"The sub?"

"Hell yeah! Buried in sand, the freaking conning tower is sticking right out of the sand. I couldn't fucking believe it, it's right there underneath us."

I pulled the tank off his back as he rubbed the salt water from his face.

"What condition is she in?" I asked.

"Can't tell, she's covered in sand, lots of sand, but looks to be more or less all there. She's listing to one side, some of the deck is gone, but the hull looks okay."

He looked up at the darkening sky. "There's not a lot of time. So get going. You take the first dive, Kevin and I'll go down after. She's just sitting there. Just follow the anchor line."

Evan helped me and Consuela with our equipment as the boat rose and dropped over ever-growing swells. First the buoyancy compensator, then double tanks, then I sat on the rail and slipped on my fins, and finally spit in my mask and adjusted it on my face. Charlie heaved a second, lighter line over the side. There was a metal basket attached.

I put the regulator in my mouth and tested it. I took it out and looked at Consuela, who had just done the same.

"Ready?"

"Let's do this."

I took a long stride off the transom and splashed into the water. Consuela was right behind me, and we were bathed in tiny bubbles.

Dense fog hovered on the sea's surface and blocked the sun and the sky, immersing us in an eerie, cloud-like place. We swam to the marker line, clipped on, and right away began the descent.

A simple movement of my lower jaw was all it took to allow pressurized air into the Eustachian tubes, equalizing the pressure. It got colder fast as darkness enveloped us from above as well as below. Consuela turned on the flashlight tethered to her wrist. In this murky world, without the tether, I realized we would have had next to no chance of finding anything, including our way back to the boat. I formed my fingers in a loose loop around the nylon cord, and didn't take my eye or my hand off it.

And then in the gray region before us, a darker form emerged. A cigar shaped shadow twenty feet below. Only when we were almost on top of it could we be sure, and then there was no mistaking it.

The submarine rested on her side in a bed of sand, like Charlie had said, tilted over 45 degrees to starboard. Our anchor had found a good hold in the sand twenty-five feet from the conning tower, which was covered in coral and

247

seaweed. I could make out the periscope and the gun deck, with the artillery piece hanging from the deck, pointing at the sea floor.

Consuela tugged at my arm and pointed at the camera tethered to my wrist. I nodded and snapped a few photos, wondering briefly if sharks were attracted to flashes. Then I noticed a large fracture behind the conning tower and we swam toward that. The deck on the stern half of the boat was peeled back like a sardine can. Death must have come quickly.

I led the way into the sub, suddenly jerking to a stop as my tank caught the twisted steel opening. "Slow down," I told myself, "breath slowly and patiently work your way in." Sharp coral scratched my ankle, the only part not covered by the wetsuit, as I pulled myself into the dark hull.

We found ourselves in a cramped compartment that housed a barnacle-encrusted motor, where a squirrelfish darted away from the light. I took more photos, the flash illuminating the rusted instruments that had once controlled the engines.

I noticed that the aft section of the compartment was blocked by sand, leaving just one way to go: towards the bow. We sank lower and picked our way through the tightest of openings into the next compartment where the diesel engines were housed, then pulled ourselves quickly through to the next bulkhead hatch into the control room where I was relieved to find there was more space. Consuela came up beside me and repeatedly tapped her watch as I clicked a few more photos.

A pair of eyeglasses rested on the rippled sand on the floor. She picked them up and rubbed them with her gloved hand as a spider crab scurried away, stirring up a

248

cloud of fine silt and sand. It paused and I followed it with the beam from my flashlight. Surprised by the light, it moved into the shadows, kicking up more sand.

I took a deep breath and continued into the blackness of the conning tower, shining my light on its walls covered in pipes and gauges, the periscope descending like a stalagmite. Forward of the control room was a passageway accessing the officers' berths, the galley, and the captain's cabin, just as the diagram I had studied earlier had shown. The galley was only just recognizable by a clutter of rusted pots and pans lying in a jumble where they had fallen, so many years before. I grabbed onto the doorway of the first cabin and pulled myself in, trying not to stir up too much silt.

On the floor, amid the clutter, sand and silt, I noticed a porcelain cup and picked it up, surprised that it looked almost new, I could make out "Wilhelmshaven" on the side of the cup. I returned to the main passageway and showed it to Consuela.

She nodded, then looked at her watch again, and at her regulator gauge. She flashed ten fingers at me, then pointed her thumb over her shoulder. Ten minutes, then we had to leave. I nodded, and we continued forward, toward the bow.

The bow, like the stern, was buried deeper than the center of the boat. Her back must have been broken in the collision with the Josiah Long. The opening through the bulkhead to the next compartment was partially blocked by sand. I started scraping away at the sand with my hands, realizing it would be a tight squeeze. Consuela tugged at my shoulder and wagged her finger. I shook my head and gave her the okay signal, then unbuckled my vest.   With the regulator still in my mouth, I carefully slid off the tank

249

and blew out the remaining air in my lungs and sank deeper, my chest resting just above the sandy bottom. There was barely enough room to squeeze through. Once through, I pulled the harness and air tank through behind me.

This was the forward torpedo room, I realized, as my flashlight illuminated the compartment. The floor was an undisturbed bed of sand. There were two torpedo tubes, but no torpedoes that I could see, just the remains of what looked like barrels and crates: rusty barrel rings and glass bottles, and pooled on the sand was the shimmering glimmer of mercury. It had been used as a cargo space, and whatever had been in the barrels had long since mixed with the sea, and drifted away, except for what remained of the mercury. I felt my heartbeat quicken, and propelled myself forward, sifting through the debris.

My concentration was broken by the sound of metal hitting metal. Consuela was tapping her flashlight against the edge of the hatch to get my attention. I looked at my watch. We had been down for twenty minutes, but we had come this far, penetrated this deep, and I couldn't bring myself to leave, not yet. The beam of Consuela's flashlight rested on a torpedo tube on the forward bulkhead. The tube's hatch was secured with a chain and padlock, both heavily corroded. I swam to it and pulled on the lock, but it was rusted shut. I unbuckled my weight belt, then exhaled to adjust my buoyancy. When I struck the weight belt against the chain, it parted easily.

Grabbing the hatch with both hands, I pulled as hard as I could. It wouldn't budge. I took a deep breath, planted my feet in the sand, and tried again. Slowly, the resistance lessened, and the hatch gave way. I aimed my flashlight into the torpedo tube and there I recognized the

250

unmistakable glint of gold.

But it was time to leave. It was past time. As quickly as I could I stuffed one bar under my vest and then filled my mesh bag with as many bars as it would hold, then heaved it through the hatch into Consuela's waiting hands. I squeezed back through the hatch, hurrying now, my ankles scratched the coral, and blood clouded the water. I barely felt it as I pulled my tank behind me and put it on.

Consuela tapped me on the shoulder and pointed at my regulator gauge. I was in the red zone, and would soon run out of air. Together, we dragged the gold through the sub, kicking up a cloud of sediment. I was breathing fast, and not getting enough air.

I heaved the sack through the sub's outer hull and dropped it to the sandy bottom. Kicking hard, I dragged it toward the nylon tether and clipped it. My lungs ached. I turned to Consuela and ran my finger across my throat. She removed her regulator and I took a short breath, and we began buddy breathing. She tugged on the nylon line and I saw the sack of gold being lifted to the surface.

We began our ascent, slowly floating up, exhaling as we rose, careful not to go faster than our bubbles. It took several minutes to reach the safety tank that dangled at twenty feet in the warm green water. There we stayed to decompress as Consuela breathed from her tank and I from the reserve tank. We could see the hull of the Pathfinder above as the gold was hoisted aboard. I took one last breath and, letting the regulator fall from my mouth, we floated toward the boat.

Pathfinder heaved up and down in the swells as I broke the surface. The weather had worsened. Consuela kicked hard and pulled herself onto the swim platform. I followed, struggling to grab hold as the boat was tossed up and down in the heavy seas. Two arms reached out to me, hooking me under the armpits and pulling me aboard. My first sight was of Evan, standing on the rocking deck, holding onto the cabin for balance.

"Harry, look out!" he shouted.

I turned to see what he meant and something hit me hard and I felt myself falling back, as if into a hole, the darkness closing in around me.

THIRTY-EIGHT

There was an all too familiar ringing and numbness in my head, and it took me a few moments to realize I could still work my jaw. When I tried to move, my head started throbbing. I lay back down, gradually becoming aware that I was on the boat, that it was moving.

"Lie still." Consuela knelt beside me.

I tried to ask what had happened, but only a guttural sound came out.

"We been hijacked," said Lopez. He was in his bunk, a bloody towel was wrapped around his hand, which he held in the air. Evan, Harry, and Kevin were crowded around the banquette.

I forced myself to sit up. "What?"

"Three men, they have guns," said Lopez. "Came up on us through the fog."

"He okay?" I asked, gesturing toward Lopez.

"He's lost some blood," answered Consuela. "Shotgun pellets."

I struggled to my feet. Through the galley porthole I could see a man on the aft deck, guarding the door. He had a pump shotgun.

"Who's driving?" I asked.

"Earl Montgomery," said Evan.

"Son of a bitch. What's he up to?" I asked.

"Getting rid of us obviously," replied Consuela. "My guess is they're taking us over the ledge into deep water, then they'll kill us and scuttle the boat. They have to kill us. No one will ever know what happened. Then they'll go

253

back and get the rest of the gold"

"Let's just tell them they can have the gold, and we won't say anything," said Evan.

"That's not going to work," I said.

I looked out the porthole again. The weather had closed in and the waves were getting bigger. Fifty yards away a large cabin cruiser held a parallel course. I recognized it as the same boat Earl had used earlier. Its pilot wore a yellow slicker, the hood blown back, his hair wet, struggling to see through the stinging spray. He maneuvered the boat closer, and I recognized him. It was Halloran. He was keeping pace with the Pathfinder.

Consuela saw my confusion and shook her head. "He's not here to help. He's been trying to get closer, so they can offload the gold. It's getting too rough," said Consuela.

I reached for the radio.

"Don't bother, they cut the wire," said Charlie.

"Cell phone?"

He shook his head.

"What about the EPIRB?" I asked, referring to the distress beacon that would alert a rescue.

"They took it with them to the other boat. That's why I think she's right, the sonsabitches mean to scuttle us," said Charlie.

"How exactly would they do that?" asked Consuela. I looked at her, regretting that I had ever involved her in this.

"Toss a flare in the engine compartment, blow us up, or just shoot us and open the bilge pump. Lost at sea, stupid enough to go out in bad weather and never heard from again, that's what they'll say."

"Where's the gold?" I asked, reaching into my vest, I felt the one bar was still there, not that it meant anything.

"What difference does it make?" replied Evan.

"I don't know," I replied.

Consuela answered. "It's still on deck, Harry, they had trouble transferring it, too rough. I don't think they counted on that."

She rummaged around in the first aid kit. It was missing everything except small Band-Aids and a roll of gauze. She wrapped a roll of gauze around my head. She did it with tenderness and care, which allowed me a moment to think.

"Charlie, any chance we can disconnect the steering in the wheel house without losing the controls on the bridge?" I asked.

"Sure."

"We can also override the throttle in the engine compartment, right, kill the engine?"

"Of course."

"Then let's do that," I said.

"How is that going to work?" asked Evan.

"There's no time to discuss it, we have to move fast."

"He's right," said Charlie. "Kevin, you go with him. I'll stand guard."

Charlie stood by the door, looking out the window. When a big wave passed, and the gunman's attention was distracted, he signaled Kevin, who opened the hatch in the floor panel. We quickly dropped into the engine compartment. A wave hit and the boat lurched, sending me tumbling. I came to rest with my neck against a tool chest that was bolted to the floor, just what I needed. Inside the chest I found a pair of pliers and a hacksaw. Kevin located the steering cable, tracing it back with his hand until he was sure it led to the pilot house. I started working on it with hacksaw, struggling for a handhold in the crowded engineering space, unable to anticipate the suddenly increasing gyrations of the boat. I sawed as fast as I could, the blade snagging on the cable when the boat lurched, or when the steering moved. I kept sawing as fast as I could.

"What's taking so long?" asked Kevin.

"This cable is strong."

"Well, hurry."

I gave it one final burst of energy and the cable parted.

"Now!" I shouted.

Kevin used the pliers to disconnect the control cable from the throttle lever. He eased the throttle back and the boat slowed to a stop. Unable to maneuver, Pathfinder was now tossed this way and that in the heavy seas. Kevin and I struggled to climb back into the cabin. As we dropped the hatch shut, a huge wave slammed into Pathfinder. For a sickening moment I thought she would capsize. Gear and galley provisions crashed down around us. Lopez fell out of his bunk. Slowly the boat rolled upright, but she was dead in the water. I noticed the waves surging up as if out of nowhere, which meant we had arrived over the shallower water.

The cabin door opened and the man with a shotgun entered, straining to keep his balance. The boat heeled sharply and he grabbed for something to hold on to. It was as good a chance as I was likely to get. I reached under my vest and took out the bar of gold. Holding onto the overhead rail, I hit him with a glancing blow off his chin.

He turned toward me, blood smeared on his mouth. I didn't hesitate. I swung as hard as I could, hitting him on the side of the head. I felt bone breaking, his legs gave out and he fell, unconscious. I dropped the bloody gold bar onto the deck.

Water now flooded into the cabin through the open

door as *Pathfinder* dropped down the face of a wave. I stepped out onto the deck where Earl stood, looking at me in surprise. The rubber boots of my wet suit gripped the deck as I lunged into him. He stumbled backwards into the transom as a wall of green water heaved up at the side of the boat. I grabbed onto the ladder and felt a massive wave washed over me, then I looked back at the deck.

Earl had vanished.

"Find him!" I yelled, suddenly aware that Charlie and Lopez were on deck. "I'll steer."

I started climbing to the bridge. The boat rocked wildly as another wave passed under. At the top of the ladder, I grabbed the wheel and felt the rudder respond. We had cut the right cable.

"Give me power! I need power!" I shouted down to the deck below. Consuela relayed the message to Kevin and after what seemed like a long time I felt the surge of the engines as the boat accelerated. I tightened my grip as we turned, slicing through the next wave. Spray drenched me, the water running off my wet suit in sheets. I took a breath as the boat stabilized, then turned when I felt Consuela beside me, squinting through the spray.

"We did it!" She screamed, wiping seawater from her face.

"Where's Earl?"

"Must have gone over. Should we go back?"

I shook my head.

"So where are we going?"

"Anywhere but here," I said, as I squinted at the compass, setting a rough course for the Bahamas.

Consuela gripped my waist. "Harry, look out!"

I looked up. Twenty feet away off our starboard rail, Halloran was bearing down on us. He had an automatic

257

weapon in his hand. I threw the helm over as a wave smashed over the bow, Pathfinder veered wildly to port and I struggled to get her back under control. When I looked up, Halloran was dead ahead, trying to turn away.

Pathfinder struck her amidships, the sound of impact was deafening as our steel hull scraped violently across the smaller craft. Then it was over. I turned to look back and saw the boat, or what was left of it, rolling on its side, sinking beneath the waves. I saw Halloran floundering in the water, waving at us for help

"Should we go back for him?" Consuela asked.

"Probably."

It was easier said that done. I was trying to steer the boat over another big roller when I heard a gunshot. Wood on the console splintered in front of me. I turned. Earl stood by the side of the wheelhouse below the bridge, his pistol raised. I threw myself in front of Consuela as he fired again. I felt something hit me and then another gun fired. Earl spun around, a look of pain and surprise frozen on his face, then sank slowly to the deck.

I looked down to see Lopez, .45 in hand, standing at the foot of the ladder, and only then did I become aware of the searing pain in my arm. Blood, mixed with water, ran down my arm, streaming across the fiberglass deck toward the scuppers. Then Consuela was beside me and I realized Pathfinder was lower in the water, she was weighted down and sluggish, and not rocking as much. I looked down at the main deck. We were sinking by the stern.

"Charlie said we're sinking. We're going down fast," said Lopez. "Tore a big hole in the hull. You okay?"

I saw Kevin and Charlie working on the fiberglass box that contained the life raft. They flipped open the top and heaved the raft onto the stern deck. Kevin tethered it to the transom and then lifted it over the side, pulling the rip cord as he let go. The orange tented raft inflated automatically. I somehow slipped down to the main deck. The boat was now awash, and I was floating. I watched as everyone climbed into the raft. Evan looked at me.

"What about the gold?"

"Leave it."

I uncleated the tether and plopped into the sea. Lopez and Kevin pulled me into the raft where I lay on the rubber bottom, listening to Consuela speak into the radio.

"May day, May day, May day, this is the motor vessel Pathfinder, Pathfinder, Pathfinder, requesting assistance."

As I drifted into unconsciousness, I heard the reassuring voice of home.

"This is Coast Guard Station Miami, go ahead Pathfinder..."

THIRTY-NINE

Consuela examined the aluminum contraption the doctors had screwed to my arm.

"Is it very painful?" she asked.

"Yes."

"How long you going to be here?"

"A week, then bed rest at home."

"Does this mean you're staying in Miami?"

"For a while."

"Well that's good. Is Aunt Mimi gonna take care of you?"

"Unless you have other ideas."

"I don't know, Harry." She had a very affectionate glint in her eyes. "No one ever took a bullet for me."

"Not even Muldoon?"

"Not even him."

After five days in the hospital, I was released into the care of Detective Sergeant Consuela Esperanza. Most of my recuperation I spent on the roof garden in a beach chair with a cooler full of beer, a book on boatbuilding, and a pair of binoculars. I was watching the comings and goings on the Miami River and wondering how I was ever going to build a boat.

On the first day of convalescence, Evan and Valerie and Uncle Mo and Aunt Mimi came by. Valerie brought chocolate, and a check for $50,000. I asked Uncle Mo to make the deposit, and I cut a check for half for Lopez.

I asked Evan about going back for the gold, but he said there had been too much blood, and now the government would want their cut, maybe all of it, which would be the final crime, but he saw no way around it. The German consulate, he said, had claimed sovereignty over the wreck as a military grave. It was getting complicated. He said he had other coals in the fire. I don't think Valerie liked it when he said that.

Over the next few days, as I recovered, Lopez and I gradually put the pieces together. One afternoon Muldoon and Lopez stopped by and drank beer with me on the roof.

"Any word on the Russians?" I asked.

"Now that Junior's out of the picture, you won't have any trouble. Juri will see to that. I think you impressed him."

"That's one thing I don't have to worry about. So you don't think Juri had anything to do with this?"

Muldoon shook his head. "Demetri and Junior were freelancing, as far as we can tell. Juri didn't like the publicity."

"So he had Junior killed?"

"Let's just say he knows how to make problems go away."

"You gonna look into that?"

"Probably not," said Muldoon.

"So who do you think killed Mink?" I asked.

"Way I figure it, Mink found out what Salisbury was on to, and told Earl. They got Junior and Demetri involved. They went to Salisbury's boat to squeeze him, only Bigelow was there."

Lopez nodded. "Wrong place, wrong time. They get into a tussle and Bigelow is killed."

"So who killed Mink?" I repeated.

"Halloran's my guess, or Earl. When Earl was a cop he worked for Halloran. When things started spinning out of control, Earl went to him for help. One of them killed Mink because they knew he would have spilled everything. He was the only link between Earl and Bigelow's murder."

"Did Halloran kill Leach?"

Muldoon shook his head. "Probably Junior, or Earl. They had to get him out of the way. I guess they figured they might as well frame Salisbury while they were at it."

I took a sip of beer.

"Things sure spin out of control, in ways you don't expect."

"You did good," said Muldoon. "You both did."

I still had one unfinished piece of business in Miami. When I was feeling up to it, I drove over to Donny's restaurant. I was taking a chance, because my arm was still in a sling, but I didn't think he'd hit a man who had a bad arm. I took a seat at the bar where I found Donny in a neck brace. He was mopping the bar with a rag.

"What are you doing here?" he asked.

"Thought we might talk."

"Come to threaten me? Warn me off?"

"No."

"Then what do you want to talk about?"

"You, and Cameron."

He eyed me for a long time, then picked up a glass and pulled me a draft beer.

"How's the neck?" I asked.

"Been worse. Your arm?"

"It's okay."

"I heard you got shot. By a cop."

"Ex-cop."

"This is one crazy town. You talked to Cameron?"

I nodded.

"So wha'd she say?"

"She said this has to stop."

He took a deep breath. "I know." He looked down and wiped his wet rag on the bar some more. "Did she say she'd see me?"

"She said maybe you could still be friends. But you have to tone it down, way down."

"She's seeing somebody else?"

"She's not seeing somebody else. But that doesn't mean she wants to see you."

"But she might?"

"Don't get your hopes up. She said you had to prove to her you could act normal. And since I don't think that's going to happen, based on what I've seen, I think you gotta find somebody else so you can get over her."

"But if I do change then she might see me?"

"She said maybe."

"I never hurt her."

"You stalked her."

"I was crazy."

"Yes, you were."

He looked at me. "So she said she'd see me?"

"She said 'maybe.'"

"Maybe's good," he said, and we drank a few more beers.

When I felt strong enough I took another drive across Alligator Alley with Lopez. Jerome Gurnee was more than happy to sell Rosy to me. He said all she needed was a little T.L.C.. I had the boat trucked to Miami, and spent three weeks working on her. I launched her on November 30th, the last day of hurricane season.

The next day I made the maiden voyage to Elliott Key. It took six hours. Call it a shake-down cruise. Rosy arrived after dark, and I set the anchor, made dinner and turned in under the stars. The next morning I woke in the V-berth. There was the mildest of ocean breezes, and Rosy tugged gently at the anchor line. Through the forward hatch I could see perfect clear blue skies. Consuela stirred beside me.

"Is it morning already?" she asked.

"So it would appear."

"Do you make coffee?"

"I do."

"My kind?"

"I brought it specially."

"Mmmmm." She wrapped her arms around me and pulled herself close. "You think of everything."

Consuela closed her eyes and slept some more. I watched her for a long while, listening to her breathe, then gently slid off the bunk and made Cuban coffee in the galley. When I returned Consuela was awake, her head sticking out of the hatch.

"There's no one here, Harry, I'm going for a swim."

"Au naturale?"

"Of course."

She turned to me.

"Are you coming?"

"I wouldn't miss it for the world."

About the author

Douglas Karlson was born and grew up in New York City. A graduate of Northwestern University and NYU's Stern School of Business, he is a newspaper editor and marketing consultant, and lives on Cape Cod.

If you enjoyed DEVIL'S REEF, be on the look-out for Harry McCoy's next adventure in COLD COMFORT. Check the author's website, www. DEKarlson.com, for updates.

What readers are saying…

"A stellar literary debut."

"Pulse-quickening…"

"…[a] swirling vortex of memorable characters, delicious settings and shocking twists of events that resists your efforts to put it down…"

"Compulsively readable!"

"Strap your air tank on extra tight for this one and remember to come up for air."

"In Harry McCoy, we have a new kind of hero -- circumstances have put this laconic, well-educated former DA beyond the emotional reach of lesser men."

"With a Russian hit-man, his marina neighbor's crazy boyfriend, and a crooked ex-cop all gunning for Harry, you can bet this is a wild ride."

"Harry McCoy promises to entertain and enthrall."

"Had there been another title in the series, I would have bought it minutes after finishing this!"

"Not only is this a worthy new literary franchise, but I'm guessing it's exactly the kind of neo-noir story that belongs on the big screen."

"It was a great read, hard to put down."

"Solid entertainment."